THE WOMEN
WHO LIVED

BBC

DOCTOR WHO

THE WOMEN WHO LIVED

Amazing Tales for Future Time Lords

CHRISTEL DEE & SIMON GUERRIER

BOOKS

CONTENTS

INTRODUCTION

"OH, BRILLIANT!"

After 55 years of TV adventures, the Doctor is beginning an exciting new chapter – in her first female incarnation.

We felt this was the perfect opportunity to celebrate the brilliant women who've appeared in *Doctor Who* over the years – because there are so many! There are the many companions who have travelled in the TARDIS – from Amy Pond, who travelled with the Doctor for longer than anyone else, to Zoe Heriot whose brilliance at maths once destroyed a whole Cyberman space fleet.

Then there are the real, historical figures the Doctor has encountered, such as the writer Agatha Christie, the Queen Nefertiti, and Locusta, court poisoner to the Roman Emperor.

We've also included many lesser known women from the Doctor's adventures, whose perspectives cast surprising new light on events in TV stories; women who've tackled feminist issues directly; and those who've demonstrated rather than spelled out their independence and agency.

We've had fun, lively arguments about who should be included, because the truth is, from the very beginning, the series has offered us compelling role models: intelligent women eager to investigate strange goings on, whatever the danger. There are simply too many brilliant, extraordinary women in *Doctor Who* but we've managed to whittle it down to our favourites.

They're not all saintly, or kind, or even on the Doctor's side
– there are some spectacular female villains in our collection –
but even the most timid of companions constantly ask questions,
challenging the Doctor to explain, justify, and do better …

Each woman we've chosen is accompanied by new artwork,
and we've encouraged our amazing illustrators to be creative
and bold – allowing some artistic licence where we thought that
was fun. We hope this offers new insights into the lives of these
women, during and beyond those times they knew the Doctor.

And we hope this book will inspire *you* – to revisit adventures
from these women's point of view, to write about and draw your
favourite characters, and to embrace the thrilling era of the
Thirteenth Doctor …

CHRISTEL AND SIMON

ACE (DOROTHY)

PLAYED BY **Sophie Aldred**

OCCUPATION **Streetwise teenager, explosives expert**

FIRST APPEARANCE *Dragonfire* (1987)

ONCE UPON A TIME, a girl created a time storm in her bedroom that swept her away to another planet.

Ace was a teenage girl from 1980s London – Perivale to be precise. She was fascinated by chemistry – even though she failed the O-level exam – and converted aerosol cans into her own brand of explosive, Nitro-9. Inevitably her exploits would often land her in trouble; she was expelled from school for blowing up the art room, and she burned down a spooky, deserted house in a fit of anger. None of this improved her relationship with her mother, which was difficult at best.

Ace worked at a till in a supermarket until a chemistry experiment in her bedroom went terribly wrong and – almost as if fate had decreed she would meet the Doctor – she found herself transported to Iceworld on the planet Svartos. There she worked as a waitress, where she met the Doctor and **Melanie Bush**, and bravely helped them battle the cold, cruel Kane. Afterwards, when Mel decided to leave the TARDIS, Ace was invited on board.

Alongside the Doctor – or "professor" as she liked to call him – Ace found a passion and a talent for battling injustice and prejudice, as well as more tangible monsters, wherever they landed. A strong improviser, she would fight fearlessly with whatever was to hand, memorably taking on the Doctor's archenemies, the Daleks, with a baseball bat, and bringing down a troop of Cybermen with nothing more than a catapult and a bag of gold coins!

It wasn't just that she was good at destroying things. Open and unprejudiced, Ace wore her heart on her sleeve. She formed close attachments with others whenever she went, from part-time werewolves to future Earth colonists. Likewise, if people disappointed her she would be swift to let them know.

As Ace travelled with the Doctor, she was growing up. She was also starting to question him – and the secrets of his past. But it was her own past the Doctor was keen to explore.

WHEN THE TARDIS LANDED in a spooky house in 1883 – the same building that the younger Ace was to burn down a hundred years in the future – she was furious that the Doctor had brought her here without warning. But in helping him solve the mystery of what had happened to leave an aura of such evil in the place, she exorcised the ghosts of her past.

Ace's darkest moments came when the TARDIS arrived in a military base in Northumbria during World War II. Without telling her, the Doctor had laid an elaborate trap for a powerful entity called Fenric; the same force responsible for the time storm that had whisked Ace away to Svartos. Ace was one of Fenric's "wolves", individuals whose lives he controlled with the ultimate aim of engineering his freedom and destroying the Doctor. While on the base, Ace met a baby that was also one of the wolves, a baby she felt a deep connection to … a baby who would grow up to become her own mother! Rocked to the core, Ace received no comfort from the Doctor, who denounced her as an "emotional cripple" – a cruel gambit he was forced to make as part of his own plans to defeat Fenric.

> " I felt like I could run forever, like I could smell the wind and feel the grass under my feet and just run forever. "

Though she and the Doctor reconciled, Ace felt a need to return home to reconnect with her old friends. But the reunion took place on a savage alien planet, where selected humans were prey for the Cheetah people. Worse, those who survived on the planet long enough would become Cheetah people themselves … and Ace soon numbered among them.

With the Doctor's help, the girl who had rebelled for the whole of her life had to learn *not* to fight, to tame the wildness inside her and channel the powers of the Cheetah people to return her friends to Earth before the planet tore itself apart. Ace came to realise more than ever that home for her meant the TARDIS with the Doctor … and who knows how long their adventures together lasted.

ADA GILLYFLOWER

PLAYED BY **Rachael Stirling**

OCCUPATION **Loyal daughter, experimental subject**

FIRST APPEARANCE *The Crimson Horror* (2013)

THERE WAS ONCE A LONELY BLIND GIRL WHO FAITHFULLY SERVED HER MAMA.

Mama was a prize-winning chemist and mechanical engineer until she returned home to Yorkshire to start a factory, providing workers with homes and a community, set out on strictly moral terms.

To packed congregations, Mama railed against the "present moral decay and the coming apocalypse", and nearby towns that were "all a-swarm with the wretched ruins of humanity."

It seemed this righteous anger had been prompted by her daughter's ruined eyesight. Mama claimed her late husband blinded Ada in a drunken rage, having seen the sin in her heart. Ada feared this meant she would not be among Mama's chosen.

Mama's new community offered salvation to the fittest and most beautiful. Mama had them preserved. She planned to flood the Earth with poison, kill imperfect humanity and start again.

However, the preservation process could go wrong, resulting in crimson-stained corpses. As a rule, these bodies were dumped in the canal, but one rejected specimen didn't die. He lay twitching and mute – until the blind girl reached out her hand.

Ada provided her "Dear Monster" with food and kindness. If he was strong enough to survive rejection, maybe he'd been spared for a reason. And if this ruined man *was* worthy of salvation, then perhaps so was she.

But no, Mama made it clear that Ada was not to be saved. Worse, the now healed Dear Monster revealed that Ada had not been blinded by her father: Mama was responsible, experimenting on her own child to find a way to protect herself from the poison she'd soon release on the world.

The Dear Monster and his friends stopped Mama from unleashing her poison – but in the process, Mama was mortally wounded. "Forgive me," the dying woman begged her daughter.

"Never," Ada said. They were not so different after all.

ADELAIDE BROOKE

PLAYED BY **Lindsay Duncan**

OCCUPATION **Astronaut, pioneer**

FIRST APPEARANCE *The Waters of Mars* (2009)

THERE WAS ONCE A GIRL WHOSE PARENTS DIED DURING A DALEK INVASION. One Dalek found her, cowering in her bedroom, but it didn't fire. It simply went away. Somehow it sensed that Adelaide Brooke was someone special who would come to play a pivotal role in future history.

After that terrifying encounter, Adelaide had starlight in her soul. She knew she would follow the Dalek into space – not seeking revenge for the loss of her parents, simply to get out among the stars. Adelaide sacrificed everything to lead the first off-world colony to Mars, leaving her daughter and granddaughter behind on Earth. Her emotional detachment made her a severe and formidable leader.

> " *I don't care who you are. The Time Lord Victorious is wrong.* "

Her baby granddaughter would one day follow her out into space, piloting the first lightspeed ship to another star. But Adelaide's granddaughter would be inspired by a tragedy, too, reaching out for the grandmother who had been killed with her crew in the destruction of the Mars colony they'd established.

Adelaide didn't want to believe it. But when her crew discovered an alien life-form was transforming her crew into mutated killers and could some day contaminate Earth, she began the procedure that would destroy the base.

The Doctor felt he couldn't turn his back on Adelaide and her crew. At the risk of all future history, he rescued those he could and took them back to Earth.

Adelaide didn't thank him. She couldn't bear to think her granddaughter might lose her future in space, or to hear the Doctor speak of his newfound power over time, of the "little people" he might save. She told him that it was wrong – and, rejecting a future that was not truly hers, took her own life.

In killing herself, she saved her granddaughter's future. And perhaps, in a way, her actions saved the Doctor from himself.

AGATHA CHRISTIE

PLAYED BY **Fenella Woolgar**

OCCUPATION **Novelist**

FIRST APPEARANCE *The Unicorn and the Wasp* (2008)

THERE WAS ONCE A WRITER OF DETECTIVE STORIES who got caught up in a mystery of her own. In 1926, she vanished, soon after discovering that her husband had been having an affair. Her disappearance was big news, and more than a thousand police officers searched for her. Ten days later, she was found safe and well at a hotel, with no memory of what happened.

It seems that the Doctor met Agatha Christie the day she disappeared, at a country house where guests were – in real life – being murdered, one by one, as if in homage to her stories. Could Agatha help solve the case?

No, she protested. Reality was different from fiction. She didn't think her stories were very good anyway.

" *How like a man to have fun while there's disaster all around him ...* "

Yet while plenty of people wrote detective stories, Agatha's brilliant mind, her talent for plotting and an understanding of the world gave them something extra. She knew about people: their passions, hopes, despair and anger. All those tiny, huge things than could turn the most ordinary person into a killer.

The killer was no ordinary person, but a giant wasp-like creature from another world. The Doctor might never have uncovered the alien intruder without Agatha's brilliant mind, for that mind was linked to the alien's own. When it died, she collapsed and lost her memory of the day's events. The Doctor dropped her off at the hotel where she would be found, putting history on its proper course.

Agatha went on to live a long and happy life, marrying again and continuing to write. If she was never sure that her books were any good, her readers thought otherwise; this best-selling novelist of all time was still being published 4,999,998,024 years after her death.

AMELIA "AMY" JESSICA POND

PLAYED BY **Caitlin Blackwood and Karen Gillan**

OCCUPATION **Kissogram, model, journalist and author**

FIRST APPEARANCE *The Eleventh Hour* (2010)

THERE WAS ONCE A GIRL WHO DIDN'T WANT TO GROW UP.

When Amelia was seven, a spaceship crashed in her garden and out clambered a hungry Raggedy Doctor. She fed him fish fingers and custard.

Amelia wasn't scared by the crashed spaceship or this strange man. But she *was* scared of the crack in her bedroom wall and the voices she heard through it at night. And there was something else … Something she couldn't remember.

Before the Raggedy Doctor could solve this mystery, he had to dash to his spaceship – saying he'd be back in five minutes.

The girl waited. He didn't return. Despite her claims, people thought she'd imagined him. Over the years, she started to think they might be right.

Twelve years later, the Raggedy Doctor turned up again at her house, still in his raggedy clothes. Amy said she didn't believe it was him, but in truth she had never stopped dreaming of the magic man she knew would one day come back …

" Twelve years. And four psychiatrists! "

Again he disappeared, and again Amy waited. Two years later, on the eve of her wedding to her childhood friend Rory, he returned and this time he took her with him in his spaceship. They had many adventures.

They learned that the crack in her bedroom wall all those years ago was one of many cracks in time and space, which could swallow people up as if they'd never existed. The girl's parents had been taken and she'd forgotten them. Then the man she'd been going to marry was lost, too.

The Raggedy Doctor helped to put things right and recover Amy's loved ones in time for her wedding day. But in doing so, the Doctor was lost himself.

However, Amy had spent so much of her life waiting for him that she *couldn't* forget. Her memories were so strong she was able to bring her Raggedy Doctor back from oblivion.

REFUSING TO CHOOSE BETWEEN the man she was going to marry and the Raggedy Doctor, she married Rory and continued to travel with the other. But the more she travelled back and forth through time and space, the more complex and mixed-up her life became. She had a child, and lost a child, then learned she'd known that child all along. The incredible events that she and her husband suffered in their travels took their toll. They almost split up.

After that, Amy and Rory travelled with the Doctor only sporadically. Amy achieved some fame as a model before becoming a travel writer. Her husband took a full-time job. Had a long-avoided ordinary life finally begun for them?

For a while it seemed they could have it both ways, stealing away from mundane reality to spend weeks in adventures, before returning to the moment they'd left.

> " *Who's there? You watch it because I am armed and really dangerous, and ... cross.* "

But the end was to come after an encounter with Weeping Angels in Manhattan, over ten years since they'd first stepped aboard the TARDIS. In a graveyard in New York in 2012, a Weeping Angel sent Amy's husband back in time to the 1930s. Amy wanted to pursue him in the TARDIS, but the Angels' feeding frenzy had scrambled the timelines round New York. Going to fetch Rory in the TARDIS, and creating another paradox, would tear the city apart.

So Amy faced a terrible choice: abandon her husband and continue to travel with the Doctor, or let the Weeping Angel send her back in time to join Rory, where they would live their lives all in a straight line, locked into the past.

For Amy, who had lived the most uncertain and unpredictable of lives, there was never any contest. She chose to follow the man she'd loved for so much of her life.

She and her husband lived happily into old age – but they could never see the Doctor again.

ANNE TRAVERS

PLAYED BY **Tina Packer**

OCCUPATION **Scientist**

FIRST APPEARANCE *The Web of Fear* (1968)

THERE WAS ONCE A BRILLIANT GIRL WHO DID BRILLIANT THINGS.

Anne's early interest in science was kindled by her father, a "mad" professor who'd discovered an Abominable Snowman, or Yeti, in Tibet in 1935, and brought it back to England. Anne was one of the few people trusted with the truth, that this Yeti was a broken robot, formerly the servant of an alien entity: the Great Intelligence. Anne's father sold the robot to a collector, keeping for himself the sphere that once powered it.

Anne, meanwhile, studied at a redbrick university, under a leading physicist and computer scientist who called her "brilliant." That brilliance led her to work in America, but then her father called her urgently back to London. His tinkering had reactivated the control sphere, and it had taken command of the Yeti.

Within weeks, this Yeti and others like it had spread a deadly web through London. The population fled but Anne and her father worked with the military to defend the city – and the Earth.

Fiercely independent, Anne refused to be patronised by the soldiers. She had inherited her father's distrust of journalists and could be suspicious of strangers. But she was also conscientious, diplomatic in her father's antagonistic affairs and ready to admit when her suspicions were wrong. When the Great Intelligence took possession of her father, she insisted that his release be included in any bargain. And despite barely surviving a brutal Yeti attack, she bravely joined the Doctor in facing them again.

It was her scientific brilliance that ultimately thwarted the alien menace, as she understood and enhanced the Doctor's design for a control unit that helped him take charge of the Yeti.

With the crisis passed, she returned to her work in America, taking her father with her.

ASHILDR / ME

PLAYED BY **Maisie Williams**

OCCUPATION **Viking, queen, soldier, highwayman, mayor**

FIRST APPEARANCE *The Woman Who Lived* (2015)

THERE WAS ONCE A GIRL WHO DIED.

Ashildr was a Viking but had always been different. She had a head full of stories she could tell very well. When the men of her village went out raiding or to battle, she'd try to find the right tale to keep them safe. Despite her strangeness, she was loved – and she loved her people.

When the Doctor and **Clara Oswald** came to her village, Ashildr discovered that the "man" claiming to be the Viking god Odin was really an alien who killed the strongest men of her village to drink their hormones. Horrified, she declared war on Odin and his warriors, although she knew there was no chance she could beat them.

Few of the remaining villagers had ever picked up a sword, but they were determined to fight and die with honour.

The Doctor had an idea and connected Ashildr to the aliens' own technology, feeding directly into the helmets they wore, and then asked her to weave one of her stories. She concocted a tale in which a huge monster attacked Odin's warriors – and the images were convincing. Clara recorded the warriors' panic, and the Doctor threatened to share the recording widely throughout the cosmos, destroying their reputation as fierce warriors. The aliens retreated and the village was saved – but in the process, Ashildr had been used up like a battery, and she died.

The Doctor refused to let that be the end of her story. He reprogrammed an alien medical kit so it would repair her, and go on repairing her ever after. Now Ashildr would *always* live. The Doctor left a second medical kit with her so that, if she wished, she could choose someone with whom to share eternity.

It would never be that simple …

She was a medieval queen, a healer who cured a village of scarlet fever, a surgeon, scientist, inventor and composer. She even founded a leper colony.

Approaching 600 years old, she lived as a man and went to war. Her long life gave her time to master archery, and she played decisive roles in the battle of Agincourt and elsewhere in the Hundred Years War.

Her head could not contain the memories of so many lifetimes. By the age of 800, she marvelled at adventures described in her diaries that she otherwise couldn't remember. She could not recall her father or the village she once died to save, or her original name. The person she'd become, she named, 'Me'.

> ❝ **Me is who I am now. No one's mother, daughter, wife. My own companion. Singular. Unattached. Alone.** ❞

Me became a highwayman – not because she needed money, but for the adventure. Yearning for new experiences, she plotted with an alien to escape to the stars, not caring that many people would suffer and die in the process, as they had such short lives anyway. The Doctor made her think again. She saved lives – and vowed to help others who, like her, were left behind in his wake.

Just before Me's 1,000th birthday, she found a hidden street in London full of alien refugees. She took charge, making the haven a stronghold by imposing strict rules, with the death penalty for those who broke them. She was soon mayor of the street.

Some 200 years later, to preserve this backwater home, Me agreed to trap the Doctor and deliver him to his own people. She didn't mean for poor Clara to die in the process, and felt real sorrow and regret …

Unable to die, Me lived on for billions of years, to the last hours of the universe. By then, she knew so much about the Doctor and his past and secrets. She guided him in his grief at losing Clara and helped him to forget her.

But Me didn't forget – and Clara wasn't quite dead. They would explore the stars together.

ASTRID PETH

PLAYED BY **Kylie Minogue**

OCCUPATION **Citizen of Sto, waitress.**

FIRST APPEARANCE *Voyage of the Damned* (2007)

THERE ONCE LIVED A WOMAN WHO DREAMED OF ANOTHER SKY.

On the planet Sto, Astrid longed to travel the stars and set foot on another world. She spent three years working at the spaceport diner but, desperate to escape, she began serving drinks aboard the cruiseliner spaceship *Titanic*. Sadly, Astrid was staff and so wasn't allowed to set foot off the ship on shore leave. Her employers, Max Capricorn Cruiseliners, claimed they couldn't afford the insurance.

The *Titanic* was orbiting a primitive planet called Earth when a mysterious new arrival, the Doctor, offered to take her as his "plus one" on the shore leave to the Earth's surface. Astrid could have got the sack but nothing was going to stop her from seeing a new sky, so she accepted.

Unfortunately, the trip was cut short due to problems on the ship. With Astrid and the Doctor back on board, the *Titanic*'s shields were down when asteroids struck, resulting in a huge loss of life.

Astrid, the Doctor and the few other survivors worked bravely together to climb through the ship, reach the bridge and save the *Titanic* – all while being pursued by deadly robots. The Doctor and Astrid got on so well that when she dared to ask if she might travel with him in his ship, he accepted.

When the Doctor was captured while confronting Max Capricorn – the owner of the company, who had sabotaged the *Titanic* to get revenge on his shareholders – Astrid used a teleportation bracelet to come to his rescue. She defeated Max by throwing his support system into the engines with a forklift truck, but at the cost of her own life.

Thanks to an emergency setting on her teleport bracelet, which rescued her molecules in homeostasis, the Doctor was able to recover Astrid, but barely long enough to say goodbye. Bereft, the Doctor scattered her atoms into space. The woman who had dreamed of travelling among the stars was now as one with them forever …

BARBARA WRIGHT

PLAYED BY **Jacqueline Hill**

OCCUPATION **History teacher**

FIRST APPEARANCE *An Unearthly Child* (1963)

SOMETIMES YOU KNOW WHEN SOMETHING ISN'T RIGHT.

Barbara knew it about one of her pupils. **Susan Foreman** was bright, but had strange gaps in her knowledge. Barbara offered to work with the girl at home, but Susan suddenly became defensive, saying her grandfather didn't like strangers.

Deciding to speak to this grandfather, Barbara got Susan's address from the school secretary and went round – to find not a house but a junkyard! She double-checked the address with the secretary, but she hadn't got it wrong.

Barbara had a terrible day worrying about what was going on. She didn't want to get the girl into trouble and she didn't want to confront her directly. Instead, she confided in another teacher, telling him her plan to return to the junkyard that evening, wait for the girl to arrive and then see what happened next.

So Barbara and her colleague Ian Chesterton watched Susan go into the junkyard. As they prepared to follow her, Barbara felt suddenly afraid – as if they were about to interfere in something best left alone.

They didn't find the girl in the junkyard, at least not at first. Instead they found a police box, humming with power as though it were alive. Then there was a grumpy old man, who refused to answer their questions or to help look for the missing girl. Barbara was sure she'd heard Susan's voice – and then there it was again, coming from the police box!

Barbara pushed her way past the old man and through the doors of the police box, becoming the first human to step inside the TARDIS.

The girl and her grandfather – a mysterious Doctor – explained that they were exiles from another world, travellers in time and space. It was an incredible story, but Barbara soon believed them. She didn't understand it, but she instinctively knew they were right.

Then, before they could stop him, the Doctor set the controls and the history teacher found herself catapulted back in time …

THROUGHOUT HER TRAVELS IN TIME AND SPACE, Barbara knew what was right. In her first trip in the TARDIS, she insisted on going back to help a gravely wounded man who'd been trying to catch and imprison Barbara and her friends! Her strong sense of fairness also helped her mediate between the Doctor and Susan when they argued, and to befriend those they met on their travels. She was calm and level-headed – usually.

Her anger erupted when they visited an Aztec city. Arguing bitterly with the Doctor that human sacrifice was not right, she boldly impersonated the goddess Yetaxa to demand that the Aztecs stopped. She wasn't successful on that occasion, and the Doctor insisted that they could never change history and shouldn't get involved. But Barbara's arguments seemed to affect the old man …

> ## " You stupid old man! Accuse us? You ought to go down on your hands and knees and thank us! "

She continued to face the brutality of history: she was sentenced to death in Paris during the Reign of Terror, sold as a slave by the Romans and kidnapped by Saracens during the Third Crusade. If she couldn't change the broad sweep of history, she found small ways to help individuals along the way.

Her knowledge of human history helped confound the Daleks when they invaded Earth, while on the planet Vortis she led an attack on the sinister Animus. Barbara's instincts could sometimes be wrong, such as when she shot and killed a friendly sandbeast she thought was attacking **Vicki**. But she was always ready to apologise, and to learn.

In her last adventure with the Doctor, she was given the chance to view any moment in history. Barbara chose a conversation between William Shakespeare and **Elizabeth I**, just to see the court and eavesdrop on real history – from a safe distance, this time.

Finally, Barbara and Ian took the risk of using a Dalek time machine to get home. It was a hard decision to leave the old man after all they had been through together. But Barbara knew it was right.

BILL POTTS

PLAYED BY **Pearl Mackie**

OCCUPATION **Canteen assistant**

FIRST APPEARANCE *The Pilot* (2017)

ONCE UPON A TIME, THERE WAS A GIRL CALLED BILL who was very curious about everything. She lived with her foster mum, Moira; her birth mother died when she was a baby and her father and other family weren't around to look after her. Moira meant well but it was often Bill who looked after her foster mum, particularly as Moira often made poor choices in boyfriends ...

Growing up, Bill had no photographs of her mum, who hated to have her picture taken. All she knew was that she and her mother looked a bit alike, so Bill made up a version of her mum in her head as someone to talk to. This imaginary Mum would offer comfort and encouragement, helping Bill through life.

" I'm a broad-minded girl ... "

Bill had always wanted to go to St Luke's, the university near where she lived in Bristol, but lacked the academic qualifications. Determined to further her education regardless, she got a job in the university canteen and started sneaking into lectures. One particular lecturer, known as the Doctor, noticed that while most people frown when they don't understand something, Bill always smiled. Sensing her raw potential, the Doctor offered to be Bill's personal tutor – for free!

Soon after this, Bill met fellow student **Heather**, and their immediate mutual attraction would become a defining factor in both their lives. Heather fell victim to a "liquid spaceship" lying dormant and in need of a pilot; sensing her desire to leave her humdrum surroundings, it absorbed and transformed her into a creature of sentient oil, one who wanted to take Bill away with her. The Doctor saved Bill and their first journeys together saw them fleeing from Heather through time and space in the TARDIS. Eventually, Bill faced Heather, bravely breaking up with her as kindly as possible in order to set her free. She assumed they would never meet again ...

BILL AND THE DOCTOR WENT ON MANY DANGEROUS and exciting adventures together and became the best of friends. She learnt lots about the universe, asking questions that, so the Doctor informed her, no one else had ever thought to ask. Bill's sensitivity and compassion – and her imaginary Mum – would even save the world from occupation by the sinister alien Monks.

Ultimately, Bill's time with the Doctor was tragically cut short. While answering a distress call from a colony ship she was shot through the chest and eventually converted into a Mondasian Cyberman. Yet her amazing mind, strengthened by her battle with the Monks, rebelled against the Cyber-programming and she was able to stay by the Doctor's side until the very end. Both of them were ready to sacrifice their lives to help save others from an attack by yet more Cybermen, simply because it was the right, and kindest, thing to do.

> ❝ *What about free will? You believe in free will. Your whole thing is ... You made me write a 3000-word essay on free will!* ❞

But the Doctor and Bill didn't die. Heather came back for Bill, transformed her into an oil-like creature like herself, and together they headed off to explore the universe, where all of creation could play backdrop to incredible and never-ending adventures ...

Meanwhile, an alien entity called the Testimony retained Bill's memories and put them in a glass avatar, which took on her form when the mortally wounded Doctor encountered them later. Despite being a physical projection of her memories, she was still very much Bill Potts and helped the Doctor to come to terms with his impending regeneration.

LADY CASSANDRA O'BRIEN.Δ17

PLAYED BY **Zoë Wanamaker**

OCCUPATION **The last "pure" human**

FIRST APPEARANCE *The End of the World* (2005)

THE CHILD WHO WOULD GROW UP TO BE CASSANDRA lived on the edge of the Los Angeles Crevice on Earth of the far future. Her father, from Texas, and her mother, from the Arctic Desert, were the last "pure" humans buried in Earth's soil.

The young Cassandra enjoyed lavish parties. At one, she met a strange man who told her she was beautiful, before collapsing and dying in her arms, an encounter that would haunt Cassandra ever after.

As she grew older, Cassandra became determined to preserve her beauty and prolong her life. She had more than 700 cosmetic procedures until she was merely a piece of skin with eyes and a mouth, stretched over a metal frame, her brain held in a jar beneath.

In the year 5,000,000,000, Cassandra was invited to the space station Platform One to witness the destruction of Earth. Short of money to pay for more procedures, she planned to sabotage the station for her own profit. But the Doctor and **Rose Tyler** foiled her plan, and Cassandra was apparently killed when her skin dried out and burst apart.

Her brain saved and her body reclaimed, Cassandra met the Doctor and Rose again 23 years later. She was hiding in the basement of a hospital on the planet New Earth, where her force-grown clone Chip stole medicines for her survival. Cassandra saw a chance to further her life by 'psycho-grafting' her mind into the bodies of, first, Rose and then the Doctor. Her plans backfired, but by placing her consciousness into others, she felt sympathy and compassion for the first time in years.

Ultimately, with her mind trapped in Chip's dying body, the Doctor took Cassandra back in time to a party in her heyday where she was just able to tell her younger self she was beautiful before Chip's body failed, and Cassandra finally died.

LADY CHRISTINA DE SOUZA

PLAYED BY **Michelle Ryan**

OCCUPATION **Aristocrat, thief**

FIRST APPEARANCE *Planet of the Dead* (2009)

LADY CHRISTINA DE SOUZA HAD A BROAD EDUCATION. She spoke fluent French, had a good understanding of physics – enough to recognise a Faraday cage when she saw one – and had strong leadership skills.

Nimble, athletic and daring, she lived for extreme experiences. So when Daddy suddenly lost his fortune – and Christina's inheritance – she became a thief.

Her robberies soon had the attention of the police, who were waiting for her when she broke into the International Gallery. Christina evaded them and simply shrugged when she saw them arrest her partner.

But the ordinary bus she escaped on drove through a wormhole, and Christina found herself on a distant planet. Other passengers were horrified but Christina declared the vast alien desert with three suns "wonderful!"

She recognised that a good leader uses her strengths – or exploits someone else's. With that in mind, she made a beeline for one particularly clever passenger, a strange man called the Doctor. Together, they organised the others to prepare the bus for a return trip to Earth before a swarm of enormous and very hungry metal stingrays arrived.

Relishing this unique predicament, she was a little reckless, showing off to the Doctor by heading down into a dark and dangerous shaft to collect a crystal she thought would help get them all home. Her criminal activities had never been about money. She craved adventure.

So when the Doctor made the stranded bus levitate, and then – as the alien swarm descended – flew it back through the wormhole to Earth ... Well, caught up in the moment, Christina kissed him.

On the ground, the police were still waiting. The Doctor couldn't bear to take her away with him in the TARDIS because he'd lost so many of those who'd travelled with him. It seemed Lady Christina de Souza would go to prison, until the Doctor helped her escape after all, and she made off in the flying bus to new adventures.

CLARA OSWALD

PLAYED BY **Jenna Coleman**

OCCUPATION **Nanny, schoolteacher**

FIRST APPEARANCE *The Snowmen* (2012)

THERE WAS ONCE A CLEVER GIRL FROM BLACKPOOL whose hunger for adventure almost equalled her need for control. Clara had planned to fulfil her late mum's dream to travel. But on the eve of her departure, she was staying with another family when *their* mother suddenly died. Knowing the weight of the young children's loss, Clara stayed to help them. She was still there a year later.

Then she met the Doctor, who offered her the chance to travel *and* continue as nanny to the children. Clara made the Doctor wait for an answer but finally agreed to join him in his ship every Wednesday. Their travels were fun and exciting, but Clara learned there was an ulterior motive for the Doctor's interest in her. Impossibly, she seemed identical to two people he'd met in his travels – both of whom had died.

> " *If you want me to travel with you, that's fine, but as me. I'm not a bargain basement stand-in for someone else.* "

When an old enemy invaded the Doctor's time stream, hoping to erase him from history, Clara followed to put things right, though she knew the time winds would probably tear her into a million pieces. In fact, she became a million echoes of the original Clara, each living an independent life somewhere in time and space. Wherever they were, these echoes worked – either directly or behind the scenes – to help the itinerant Doctor.

Inside the Doctor's time stream, the original Clara saw all his lives and came to know him better than anyone else. That helped her to avert a catastrophe in his darkest hour, on the last day of the Time War. Instead of letting him destroy the Daleks and his own people, she reminded him who he was, and who he wanted to be. The Doctor spared his own people – and, again thanks to Clara, they in turn granted the Doctor another cycle of regenerations.

FOR ALL CLARA KNEW ABOUT THE DOCTOR IN HIS DIFFERENT LIVES, the Twelfth Doctor came as quite a shock. When he asked if she thought him a good person, at first she couldn't answer.

She continued to travel with him, but it was difficult to juggle her exciting adventures alongside a new job as a teacher. She also started to date one of her colleagues, Danny Pink, a former soldier haunted by tragic loss. He and the Doctor didn't get on, so Clara told each of them that she'd given up the other, thinking that way she could keep both.

When her boyfriend suddenly died in an accident, Clara was stricken with guilt and angry at the cruel loss. She tricked and threatened the Doctor, desperate for his help – which he gave willingly, anyway. They couldn't save Danny, but Clara selflessly didn't reveal this to the Doctor, knowing he had a chance to go home to his own people.

66 Let me be brave. 99

In fact, he'd lied, too, so she wouldn't feel guilty about leaving him. When they realised, she rejoined him in the TARDIS – but something had changed. She now embraced danger a little too keenly.

Finally, in a hidden street in London, her clever scheme to save a friend from a death sentence backfired and the sentence was transferred to Clara. Aghast, she bravely accepted her fate rather than let anyone else be harmed. She even begged the Doctor not to seek revenge for her death.

The Doctor brought her back, breaking all the rules of time to save her – but an ancient Time Lord prophecy warned of dire consequences for the rest of time and space if they remained together.

Reluctantly, the Doctor sought to prevent this by making Clara forget him and all that they had shared. But she had already lost so much she could never agree to that. Forthright to the end, she turned the tables so that it was the Doctor who forgot *her*. Then, with a companion by her side, she took the controls of her own TARDIS and set out to explore the stars.

DONNA NOBLE

PLAYED BY **Catherine Tate**

OCCUPATION **Office temp**

FIRST APPEARANCE *Doomsday* (2006)

THERE ONCE LIVED A WOMAN WHO COULDN'T ALWAYS SEE THE BIGGER PICTURE, but became the most important person in all creation.

Donna didn't always get on with her mum, who constantly nagged her and made her feel clumsy and small. But her grandfather defended her and, on clear nights, Donna would join him stargazing and share her dream of reaching the stars.

> " *Donna, by the way. Donna Noble, since you didn't ask. I'll have a salute.* "

That longing to escape meant Donna couldn't quite settle on what she wanted to do. She had many temporary jobs before joining security business HC Clements. There, she fell in love with the charming head of HR and was soon making plans for their wedding – unaware that, all along, he was secretly mutating her body chemistry at the behest of the wicked Empress of the Racnoss. The Empress wished to bring about the awakening of her spidery children buried deep within the Earth. The infant creatures would have fed on all humanity, so the Doctor was forced to drown them all. Donna dragged him away from the terrible scene, and seeing her compassion, he offered her the chance to join him in the TARDIS. But now she'd seen the darkness in him, Donna was wary and declined.

Instead, she quit temping and travelled to Egypt, but soon felt bored. Hoping to find the Doctor again, she began investigating unexplained events. Lo and behold, they met up in the offices of Adipose Industries, who were birthing alien creatures out of human fat.

With the menace defeated, the Doctor again invited Donna aboard the TARDIS. She not only accepted but had her bags already packed and waiting. She had just one request: that the Doctor materialise the TARDIS high above the Earth so Donna could wave down to her stargazing grandfather, who shared her delight that she'd fulfilled her dream.

DONNA'S AMAZING EXPERIENCES on her many travels showed her that she was stronger and smarter than she'd ever realised. Whether sleuthing with **Agatha Christie**, saving innocents from the fires of Pompeii, fighting Sontarans or solving conundrums on distant colony worlds, Donna displayed an inner strength and resilience that the Doctor knew he could always rely on. She loved travelling the universe with him. But their most astounding adventure was, for them both, literally life-changing – and, for Donna, her last.

The Earth was one of many planets stolen by Davros, creator of the Daleks, to power a Reality Bomb, which would eradicate everything in the universe. When the Doctor was shot by a Dalek, Donna was affected by regenerative energy and became half-human and half Time Lord. Endowed with brilliance and agility – and her already excellent typing skills from her temping days – she was able to turn the tables on Davros by disabling the Reality Bomb with just moments to spare. She was also smart enough to guide the Doctor's friends as they worked the controls of the TARDIS together in order to return Earth to its proper place in the cosmos.

> ❝ Donna! I'm a human being. Maybe not the stuff of legend, but every bit as important as a Time Lord, thank you. ❞

Tragically, this Time Lord intelligence would soon burn up her human brain. The only way the Doctor could save her was to wipe her memories of him – all that experience that had made her a more confident, accomplished and happier person. She became the woman she'd been before: not seeing the bigger picture, unable to settle down.

But she did find love again, and – although he couldn't speak to her in person – the Doctor solved her money troubles with the wedding gift he sent: a winning ticket for the National Lottery. After all, she deserved it. Because while, for her own sake, Donna could never remember her travels with the Doctor, there were whole civilisations safe in the sky because of her.

DOROTHEA "DODO" CHAPLET

PLAYED BY **Jackie Lane**

OCCUPATION **Orphan**

FIRST APPEARANCE *The Massacre of St Bartholomew's Eve* (1966)

THERE WAS ONCE A GIRL WHO DIDN'T LIKE HER LIFE IN LONDON. Dodo had no parents; her mum died while Dodo was still at school and she was brought up by an indifferent great aunt.

One day, Dodo witnessed an accident where a boy was hurt. She rushed to a police box to call for help, and stumbled into the TARDIS just as it was departing. Dodo wasn't too alarmed to leave her old life behind. There were strange destinations to explore, lots of questions to ask – and the TARDIS wardrobe to raid for ever more odd clothes!

It was fun, though Dodo denied she was ever "playing". In fact, she took games seriously, outraged by the cheating of the Celestial Toymaker's minions.

" Ain't it fab? "

Her intelligence matched her enthusiasm: arriving in a strange jungle, she was quick to spot that the plants and animals all came from different continents on Earth. She could be overly confident, but also modest about her abilities. When the Doctor called her a "wizard of the keys" in playing the piano, she responded merely that she'd "have a bash" – but her audience were so impressed they demanded she play again.

Perhaps she never quite said what she truly felt for the dashing young space pilot she and the Doctor travelled with. Steven Taylor's decision to leave the TARDIS must have struck a chord with Dodo; when, soon afterwards, she arrived in London in her own time she enthused, "It's marvellous to be back." Quickly making friends with **Polly**, another trendy Londoner, Dodo admitted that she felt out of touch – as if she regretted how long she'd been away.

While the Doctor wanted to battle evil, Dodo wanted to get back to ordinary life. Hypnotised by an evil computer, then set free from its control by the Doctor, Dodo was packed away to convalesce and decided not to return to the TARDIS. She sent him a letter to say so, along with her love.

QUEEN ELIZABETH I

PLAYED BY **Vivienne Bennett, Angela Pleasance, Joanna Page**

OCCUPATION **Queen of England**

FIRST APPEARANCE *The Chase* (1965)

ONCE THERE WAS A QUEEN OF ENGLAND who enjoyed a picnic with her "Dearest Love", an alien called the Doctor. He proposed, she accepted and they promptly married. Then he abandoned her.

Elizabeth had always been fierce. She had lived a tough life and thought nothing of concealing a dagger with which to defend herself. On the day the Doctor proposed in 1562, she joked about having people executed, and fought and killed a Zygon that had the impertinence to assume her image. She then took its place, impersonating the monster-in-disguise so as to learn what the aliens were up to in her kingdom.

She wasn't unduly concerned by the Doctor's alien nature, or by two different versions of him turning up out of thin air. By then she'd already fought monsters and seen inside the TARDIS. She spoke confidently of the Time War and the Zygons' mission to occupy Earth.

> ❝ *I may have the body of a weak and feeble woman – but at the time, so did the Zygon.* ❞

Sometime after the Doctor abandoned her, Elizabeth located the three-dimensional painting known as *Gallifrey Falls* or *No More*, and recognised its importance to her dearest love. But she also knew her duty, and that the Zygons would be back to threaten her country, centuries after her death. So rather than use the painting to lure the Doctor back into her presence, she left instructions for how it should be presented to him by her successors.

She signed off the instructions kindly, wishing him well. But when still he didn't come back to her, her heart turned against him. Elizabeth didn't see the Doctor again for 37 years, by which time she'd decided that this pernicious man – who, if anything, seemed younger now than when she'd first met him – was her sworn enemy. "Off with his head!" she demanded.

DR ELIZABETH "LIZ" SHAW

PLAYED BY **Caroline John**

OCCUPATION **Scientist**

FIRST APPEARANCE *Spearhead from Space* (1970)

ELIZABETH SHAW WAS NOT PLEASED to be summoned to London on secret government business. After all, she had an important research programme at Cambridge. But UNIT needed a good scientific all-rounder to help them investigate strange goings on. She was an expert in meteorites and had qualifications in medicine and physics, among other subjects.

She made no secret of her displeasure, and could be impatient with people she considered foolish. Yet she quickly got to work studying a strange fragment of meteorite that had crashed to Earth early that morning. Then into her lab strolled the Doctor, an alien scientist who she soon recognised had greater knowledge and experience. They quickly hit it off and she let him call her "Liz" – she was "Miss Shaw" to almost everyone else.

" I deal with facts, not science-fiction ideas. "

They made a good team. Together, they built a machine to defeat the Auton invasion, and Liz could even fix it quickly when it went wrong. She helped the Doctor develop a cure for a killer disease spread by the Silurians, and a device for communicating with ambassadors from Mars. Together, they even successfully linked up the TARDIS console to a nuclear reactor.

For all her skills, she could be gullible, falling for a trick by the Doctor to recover the TARDIS key, and again when he sent her off to double-check a computer so she wouldn't stop him conducting a dangerous test. She was far more sceptical when it came to scientific matters, but she accepted in the end that the Doctor really could travel in time and space, even though he only ever transported her a few seconds into the future.

Ultimately, Liz returned to Cambridge, having decided she was too qualified to be the Doctor's assistant. But she never lost contact with that secret world. When last heard of, a few years ago, she was up on a secret Moonbase, continuing her brilliant work with UNIT.

QUEEN ELIZABETH X

PLAYED BY **Sophie Okonedo**

OCCUPATION **Queen**

FIRST APPEARANCE *The Beast Below* (2010)

LIZ TEN, BORN DURING THE LATE 30TH CENTURY, grew up on stories of the Doctor meeting her ancestors, **Elizabeth I** and **Victoria**.

At 40, Liz became queen of the United Kingdom. She was very popular with her people. But 10 years later, her government kept secrets from her and people lived in fear in her kingdom – now a starship fleeing the burning Earth.

Liz exposed the greatest secret using a glass of water, finding it remained still when the engines of a large spaceship ought to cause vibration. So how were they travelling? She took to the streets, incognito in velvet cape and an antique mask, to find answers.

> ❝ **I'm the bloody queen, mate. Basically, I rule.** ❞

Then she recognised the Doctor, who'd spotted the same clues. She helped him investigate and, together, they exposed the awful truth: the people of the UK had built their city on the back of a Star Whale, keeping it in agony.

Liz vowed to stop this maltreatment yet releasing the whale would destroy the starship and kill all her subjects. The only other option was for Liz to forget – and it turned out she'd chosen to forget many times before. Liz wasn't 50 years old, more like 300. She hadn't aged as her body clock had been slowed.

The Doctor's friend **Amelia Pond**, horrified by her own decision to forget the awful truth, grabbed Liz's hand and pressed it against the button that would release the Star Whale. But the starship wasn't destroyed. The creature was still willing to transport Liz and her people, despite its suffering.

Later, Liz gave her mask to the Doctor, a sign that there would be no more secrets in her kingdom. She was apparently still on the throne almost 2,000 years later, allowing **River Song** to take a painting from the Royal Collection to help the Doctor in the year 5145!

PROFESSOR EMILIA RUMFORD

PLAYED BY **Beatrix Lehmann**

OCCUPATION **Archaeologist**

FIRST APPEARANCE *The Stones of Blood* (1978)

PROFESSOR EMILIA RUMFORD WAS THE AUTHOR of *Bronze Age Burials in Gloucestershire*, the definitive work on the subject – even if she said so herself. She was still working in her old age, conducting a topographical, geological, astronomical and archaeological survey of the stone circle known as the Nine Travellers on Boscombe Moor in Cornwall.

To carry out this research, she lodged at the cottage owned by Vivien Fay, and persuaded the young woman to assist in her work. The Doctor's friend **Romana** was also soon enlisted, with Emilia a jovial leader who supplied her workers with sausage sandwiches and plenty of tea.

Emilia could be disparaging to men, dismissing her male colleagues as fools – at least until the Doctor came into her life. They worked together to uncover the mystery of the stone circle, Emilia finding it "exciting" as things got more dangerous and strange.

> ## "Nobody's ever had to question the quality of my research."

The stones turned out to be deadly living creatures, and Emilia's friend Vivien a 4,000 year-old alien criminal on the run. Emilia was out of her depth, yet her brilliant mind valiantly tried to keep up. She understood Einstein's Special Theory of Relativity well enough to grasp the implications of hyperspace, which housed a prison from which Vivien had escaped. Under the supervision of the Doctor's robot dog K9, Emilia repaired the Doctor's teleportation device in time to rescue him and Romana.

Vivien was recaptured and sentenced to perpetual imprisonment. Despite the woman's lies and evil plans, Emilia felt sorry for her. She was also unsure how to write up her survey of the stone circle, given the extraordinary events she'd witnessed. "I do have my academic reputation to consider," she said.

DR GRACE HOLLOWAY

PLAYED BY **Daphne Ashbrook**

OCCUPATION **Senior cardiologist**

FIRST APPEARANCE *Doctor Who* (1996)

THERE WAS ONCE A GIRL WHO FEARED DYING. She had a childish dream that she would be able to hold back death, and this led to her pursuing a career in medicine.

She became an accomplished heart surgeon, with her colleagues referring to her as "Amazing Grace", and her interest in pioneering new medical techniques got her on to the board of trustees at the Institute of Technological Advancement and Research.

Grace had a deeply romantic side too; opera could move her to tears, and when a strange but good-looking man she'd only just met suddenly kissed her, she asked him to kiss her again. When he then convinced her that he could hold back death – and fulfil her childish dream – she was ready to risk arrest to help him steal a beryllium chip, even holding a police officer at gunpoint.

> ❝ *Oh great. I finally meet the right guy and he's from another planet.* ❞

She was amazed by the vast interior of the Doctor's TARDIS, but also understood much of the theoretical physics behind it. That knowledge soon saved the world: with the Doctor indisposed, it was up to Grace to rewire the TARDIS, rerouting power to put the ship in a temporal orbit.

This foiled the evil scheme of the Master, who killed Grace for what she'd done. But the properties of the temporal orbit, and perhaps some element of the TARDIS, too, brought her back to life. Finally, she'd fulfilled her dream and held back death, which no longer held any fear for her.

When the Doctor offered to take Grace with him in the TARDIS to explore time and space, she turned the tables and asked him to stay with her instead in San Francisco – and he was tempted. They kissed one last time. Then he was gone, and Grace went on to great things as a surgeon, holding back death for other people.

GWYNETH

PLAYED BY **Eve Myles**

OCCUPATION **Domestic servant, psychic**

FIRST APPEARANCE *The Unquiet Dead* (2005)

THERE WAS ONCE A GIRL WHO HEARD VOICES.

Gwyneth grew up in Cardiff, near the weak point in time and space known as the "rift." From a young age, she was able to see into people's thoughts, sense the future and commune with ghosts. Her mum told her to keep her abilities secret.

When Gwyneth was 12, her parents died of flu, but her strong faith told her she would see them again, when her own time came. She was paid a generous amount to work for undertaker Mr Sneed, keeping house and helping with the disposal of the dead. He also made use of her psychic abilities, against her better judgment.

Each night, the voices grew stronger. Then the dead bodies Mr Sneed tended started coming to life. Gwyneth helped Sneed recover them – using her powers to find them – and lied to other people to protect their secret. That wasn't easy for a timid, God-fearing girl who had such a sense of right from wrong.

When the Doctor wanted to hold a séance to reach the ghostly voices directly, Gwyneth assisted, revealing the ghosts to be alien beings who'd lost their physical form.

Gwyneth was determined to help her "angels", believing that her late mother had sent them to her. Smarting at the thought she saw in **Rose Tyler's** head – that Gwyneth was stupid – she opened the link and let her angels through.

But the voices had lied. They wanted to take the bodies of the living as well as the dead. Betrayed, Gwyneth wasn't strong enough to send them back, but she could hold them in Sneed's house while she burned it down.

The Doctor would have stopped her, but Gwyneth had already been killed by her angels and was living on only while the link remained open. The Doctor thanked her before she lit a match and the house erupted in flames, saving her world.

RIGHT HONOURABLE HARRIET JONES, MP

PLAYED BY **Penelope Wilton**

OCCUPATION **MP for Flydale North, Prime Minister**

FIRST APPEARANCE *Aliens of London* (2005)

HARRIET JONES, MP, NEVER EXPECTED TO HOLD HIGH OFFICE. She just did what she could for her constituents and cared for her mother. When her mother was admitted to hospital, Harriet saw a way to improve the NHS system and made an appointment with the Prime Minister.

Unfortunately, the meeting was timed for the day an alien spaceship crashed into the Thames.

Harriet didn't give up. Slyly but politely, she brought a junior secretary tea in the hope he'd help her, before sneaking into the Cabinet Room to leave her proposal on the PM's desk. There she discovered the wicked, farting aliens who had murdered the Prime Minister.

Soon, Harriet was helping **Rose Tyler** and the Doctor counter an alien invasion. But when the Doctor wouldn't risk Rose's life to stop the invasion, Harriet showed inner steel, ordering him to put the greater good first. He fired missiles at Downing Street, where the aliens were based – and where he, Rose and Harriet were hiding, too.

They survived, and Harriet was soon out reassuring the public. Her effectiveness saw her elected Prime Minister and thus began a "Golden Age" for the country.

When more aliens invaded, Harriet stood her ground against reporters, the US President and the invaders. Even when the Doctor repelled the aliens, Harriet showed steely resolve, giving orders to destroy the retreating ship.

The Doctor was horrified, but she was unrepentant: Earth's people needed defending. Although she lost her position, she went on to develop a subwave communication network that proved vital in defeating the Daleks. Harriet knew it would lead the Daleks to her, but she refused protection, insisting it be offered to other people.

Even the Daleks recognised this diligent, defiant leader – before they exterminated her.

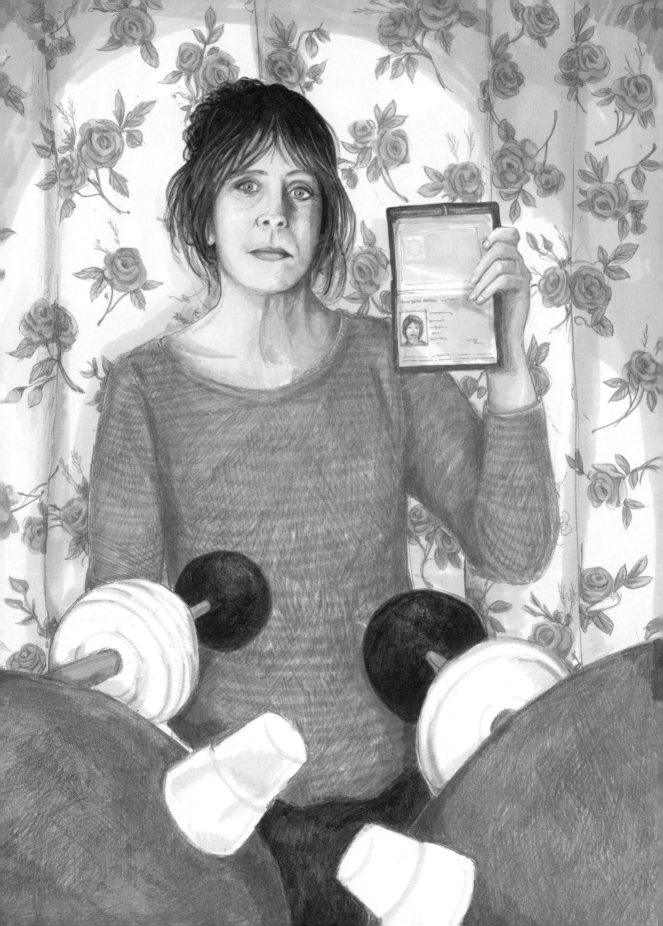

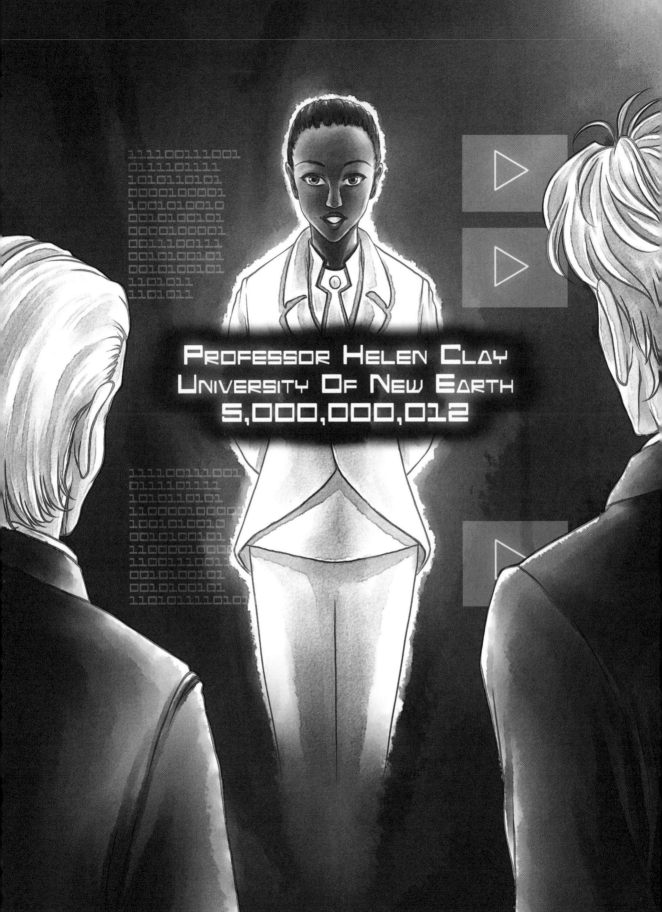

PROFESSOR HELEN CLAY

PLAYED BY **Nikki Amuka-Bird**

OCCUPATION **Scientist**

FIRST APPEARANCE *Twice Upon a Time* (2017)

HELEN CLAY WAS A BRILLIANT SCIENTIST based at the University of New Earth in the galaxy M87. In the year 5,000,000,012, she perfected a system to combine time travel with memory extraction techniques.

Her organisation, the Testimony Foundation, used this system to roam all of time and space, find people who were about to die and then clone their memories. The people would die as they must, but their memories – their essential being – would be saved for ever, in a process that left them oblivious to it even happening.

The memories were stored in a databank, accessed through an interface resembling a person made of glass. Helen's ingenious system didn't just parrot the recorded voices of the dead; the simulacrum could behave and respond as the dead person had, and look exactly like them.

" Not everything's evil, Doctor. "

The effect was to provide direct access to the minds of the dead, hearing them speak as they would have in life. Helen herself called the system "Heaven on New Earth", and the Doctor came to understand its boundless potential for studying and understanding history – and bringing comfort in the form of old, lost friends, resurrected.

The default version of the glass avatar was based on Helen's own features. Ironically, beyond this, we don't know much about Helen Clay. She probably wasn't from New Earth originally; it was discovered and colonised only after the destruction of the old Earth, 12 years before Helen perfected her system.

Some 27 years later, a virus that mutated inside a chemical compound called Bliss killed most of the inhabitants of New Earth in just seven minutes. We don't know if Helen Clay was among the millions who died. But however her life ended, she would live on in the system she'd already created.

THE HOSTESS

PLAYED BY **Rakie Ayola**

OCCUPATION **Hostess**

FIRST APPEARANCE *Midnight* (2008)

THERE WAS ONCE A WOMAN who looked after the tourist passengers on a Crusader Tours space truck during the four-hour journey to the Waterfall Palace on a strange planet of fused diamond orbiting an X-tonic star.

Perhaps the Hostess didn't share her passengers' enthusiasm for the 100,000 metre high crystal ravine, but then she'd made this journey many times before. She simply got on with her job.

When the truck broke down in the deadly radioactive wilderness, the Hostess remained calm, reassuring her passengers with the kind lie that the stop was perfectly routine … until the driver and mechanic were ripped from the front of the truck by some unseen alien menace, which then seemed to infect a passenger, Sky Silvestry. The Hostess was the first to suggest that they throw her off the truck to her certain death. The passengers concurred until challenged by the Doctor. Could they really kill someone, he asked?

"I'd do it," said the Hostess.

She had assessed the risk of this infection spreading to the remaining passengers – and to the inhabitants of the planet – and decided that extreme action was necessary. The Doctor protested but then the Hostess seemed prepared to throw him out, too. Who was he anyway? She didn't know *his* full name, only that he'd joined the tour at the last minute.

Her suspicions spread to the other passengers, who turned on the Doctor. They began to think he had infected Sky, that *he* should be the one to go.

Then the Hostess had doubts. From close study – and cold, intelligent logic – she was certain that Sky was affecting the Doctor, not the other way round. But when the passengers would not listen there was only one course of action. The Hostess took hold of Sky, opened the emergency door, and both were swept to their deaths.

She had saved the Doctor and the other passengers. And they'd never even known her name.

HUR

PLAYED BY **Alethea Charlton**

OCCUPATION **Consort to the leader of a primitive tribe**

FIRST APPEARANCE *An Unearthly Child* (1963)

LONG AGO, THERE WAS A WOMAN WHO WAS COLD AND HUNGRY. The old leader of her tribe had died without sharing the secret of how to make fire, not even with his son, Za.

Hur was a shrewd woman who understood people's motives. Ambitious, she wanted Za for her mate, but tribal law made it her father's decision and he wasn't convinced. Hur told her father that Za would be a strong leader. "If you give me to him, he will remember and always give you meat."

Za himself heeded Hur's counsel, and with her help caught out his rival when he lied. Hur still had to be careful with her cleverness. The rival was prepared to kill in his efforts to become leader, and even Za could turn violent.

Then the tribe met strangers who knew the secret of fire. When the strangers escaped, Hur urged Za to pursue them, even into the forest where bears and tigers roamed. It was a dangerous gamble but she understood that knowledge of fire would leave them unassailable among the tribe. Bravely, she followed Za, urging him ever on.

So it was her fault when Za was gravely wounded by a beast. She wept bitterly, but then, to her amazement, the strangers came back to help. Hur was fearful, and jealous when the women tended Za's wounds.

Helping Za meant the strangers were recaptured by the tribe. They made fire for him, which made him undisputed leader. Hur's standing changed, too. The once dutiful daughter now snapped back at her father when he criticised Za. She would not listen to the strangers' appeals to be freed; after all, they had nothing left to bargain with since they'd shared their secret.

The strangers escaped again, and this time did not return. But the fire they had brought to the tribe would burn on. Hur lived long and warm as consort to the tribal chief.

IDRIS (THE TARDIS)

PLAYED BY **Suranne Jones**

OCCUPATION **Humanoid, hosted the consciousness of the Doctor's TARDIS**

FIRST APPEARANCE *The Doctor's Wife* (2011)

ONCE UPON A TIME, there was a woman who became so much bigger on the inside.

It had been love at first sight. In a repair shop on the planet Gallifrey, the Doctor snuck into a broken old TARDIS with a faulty navigation system. But this ship was, he said, the most beautiful thing he'd ever known. He stole her – and she stole him.

Together, they explored all the marvels and mysteries of space and time, from beginning to end. Even though she was a machine, he'd talk of her as being alive and being a she. And then, all too briefly, she was …

Her name was, or had been, Idris, and she lived in a junkyard on an asteroid outside the universe, under the control of a malevolent cosmic entity called House. House lured TARDISes to his domain to feed on them.

> " *Goodbye. No, not goodbye, what's the other one?* "

When House lured what was apparently the last TARDIS – the Doctor's – to the junkyard asteroid, he sought to place his own consciousness inside the ship to seek out new feeding grounds. Before he could do so, he had to draw out the matrix of the Doctor's TARDIS, which he placed into the body of Idris, squeezing out whatever soul or personality had been there before. House escaped into the wider universe with two of the Doctor's friends, **Amy** and Rory, trapped on board, leaving Idris with the soul of the TARDIS inside her.

Possessing a humanoid body was confusing for the TARDIS, especially at first. Her sense of time was all back to front, so she greeted people with a cheery, "Goodbye!" and replied to things that hadn't happened yet. Being a woman and having feelings was confusing, too. But finally she could speak directly to her beloved thief …

IDRIS, WITH THE MATRIX OF THE DOCTOR'S TARDIS INSIDE HER, was locked up by the other inhabitants of the asteroid until her thief, the Doctor, came to her rescue … and finally realised who she was.

For the first time in all the centuries they had known one another, the Doctor and the TARDIS could talk. He blamed her for not always taking him where he'd wanted to go. "No," she countered, "but I always took you where you *needed* to go."

The Doctor, of course, needed to get to Amy and Rory on board the House-possessed TARDIS. Idris was ready to take him anywhere, as always. Firstly, she advised the Doctor that they use spare TARDIS parts from the junkyard to build a new console to chase after House. With a touch of Idris's TARDIS energy, they headed off through the vortex. Idris then made a psychic connection with Rory and gave him directions to a secondary control room so that they could lower the TARDIS's shields and the Doctor and Idris could land inside.

> " *I'll always be here, but this is when we talked, and now even that has come to an end … I just wanted to say hello.* "

The Doctor managed to trick House into transporting them into the main control room. But by now, Idris's mortal body was struggling to contain the colossal energies of the old TARDIS. She finally collapsed and died. The Doctor was heartbroken. But the soul of the TARDIS wasn't destroyed with her; she had simply left Idris's mortal body. Now she merged back with the TARDIS's mechanical systems, ejected House from the ship, and spoke to the Doctor for one final time. It wasn't goodbye. She would always be there for him, so she simply used her last chance to talk to say something she'd always wanted to say: "Hello, Doctor. It's so very, very nice to meet you."

THE INQUISITOR

PLAYED BY **Lynda Bellingham**

OCCUPATION **Gallifreyan judge**

FIRST APPEARANCE *The Trial of a Time Lord* (1986)

THERE WAS ONCE A POLITICALLY ADEPT and well-respected figure in the judiciary of Gallifrey. She was asked by the High Council of the Time Lords of Gallifrey to oversee an independent inquiry into the behaviour of their former president, the Doctor. He was accused of breaking the First Law of Time by continually interfering in the affairs of other planets.

The Inquisitor conducted the inquiry with professional detachment, following all due procedures. She repeatedly offered to appoint a court defender to represent the Doctor, but he declined. She repeatedly – and patiently – kept both the Doctor and the prosecuting counsel, the Valeyard, to the point as they presented evidence from the Matrix, the Time Lords' repository of knowledge.

" Sit down and shut up. "

The inquiry soon became a trial and the Doctor found himself facing the death penalty. The Inquisitor was subsequently outraged to discover that sensitive portions of evidence had been censored and redacted by the High Council. She could not carry out her job properly without access to all material, she argued, but declined to view it privately as this would be unfair to the Doctor.

The evidence in the trial grew more dramatic, and the outbursts in the trial chamber more frequent, but the Inquisitor remained matter-of-fact in her dealings and crisp in her judgements. Ultimately, however, the Doctor's suspicions that he was being set up for a fall were proven right, and the Inquisitor came to see that they had both been pawns in a High Council plot to hand power – and the Doctor's remaining regenerations – over to the Valeyard. The conspiracy was exposed and stopped. All charges against the Doctor were dismissed, and the Inquisitor invited him to stand once again for president.

He had a better idea. The Time Lords needed someone scrupulously firm but fair. If the Inquisitor were to stand, he said, he would vote for her.

JACKIE TYLER

PLAYED BY **Camille Coduri**

OCCUPATION **Rose Tyler's mum**

FIRST APPEARANCE *Rose* (2005)

ONCE UPON A TIME, THERE WAS A WIDOWED MUM CALLED JACKIE who brought up her daughter, **Rose Tyler**, as best she could. Jackie could be selfish, even a bit controlling, but she always thought she had Rose's best interests at heart.

Then Rose got a job in a department store, which gave her airs and graces in Jackie's eyes. One day, the department store burned down. Thankfully, Rose was unhurt. But soon afterwards, Jackie was in town late-night shopping when shop window dummies came to life and began killing people! She barely escaped with her life.

Not long after that, Rose disappeared without trace. Jackie was bereft, left in limbo, not knowing what had become of her daughter – until one year later, Rose returned out of the blue, accompanied by a stranger, the Doctor. Jackie was furious that he'd taken Rose away, and gave him a huge slap around the face. It was not to be the last clash between them over Rose's safety.

Inevitably, Jackie was quickly swept up into their crazy world, and was soon attacked by a deadly Slitheen, in her own kitchen! She found it hard to cope with the idea that Rose was happy leading such a dangerous life, and that she would be gone for months in the TARDIS without a word. When the Doctor sent Rose home in the TARDIS during a particularly dangerous adventure, Jackie loved him for it. But seeing her daughter so upset, Jackie tried to help her return to his world, borrowing a tow truck from a male friend in a bid to force open the TARDIS's systems.

Jackie was one of the first people to encounter the Doctor after he regenerated, and helped him to recover. Their relationship after that was much warmer.

In the end, she journeyed to a parallel world where her late husband was still alive. She stayed, they got back together and had another baby: Neil, a brother for Rose. But when the Daleks invaded the original Earth, Jackie was ready to help fight back.

LADY JENNIFER BUCKINGHAM

PLAYED BY **Jane Sherwin**

OCCUPATION **Aristocrat, Women's Volunteer Reservist**

FIRST APPEARANCE *The War Games* (1969)

THERE WAS ONCE A BRAVE WOMAN, keen to do her bit for the war effort.

During World War I, Lady Jennifer Buckingham joined the Women's Volunteer Reserve, a group that had been established by a leading suffragette. Before the war, this strident woman had campaigned vigorously to change the law so that women could vote in elections, and now she saw a chance to organise a prominent role for women.

The WVR was efficient and disciplined, its members trained in drill, signalling, motor mechanics, cooking and nursing. It offered useful and interesting roles for women but was expensive to join. As a result, its members were soon a mixture of dedicated feminists like those who'd established the group, and wealthy, upper-class women such as Lady Jennifer.

In 1917, the WVR had Lady Jennifer working in France, sometimes as a nurse in a hospital a safe distance from the fighting, and sometimes driving an ambulance through the thick of the action. Out in no man's land, there was the constant threat of bombardment by shells, capture by enemy soldiers and the enemy's devastating new weapon: mustard gas. Lady Jennifer met these dangers with pluck and good cheer.

However, she also thought she might be suffering from "shell shock", better known today as post-traumatic stress disorder. When she met the Doctor and his friends, her intelligence and courage helped reveal the awful truth: that she and the soldiers around her weren't on Earth any more, but were fighting – and dying – in a war game controlled by wicked aliens.

Jennifer bravely joined the resistance against these aliens. She was all set to lay siege to the aliens' headquarters despite what the men around her thought about a woman going into battle. However, men wounded in the games also needed medical attention and, with good grace, Jennifer agreed to help. She was later returned to Earth by the Doctor's own people.

JENNY
(THE DOCTOR'S DAUGHTER)

PLAYED BY **Georgia Moffett**

OCCUPATION **Soldier, generated anomaly**

FIRST APPEARANCE *The Doctor's Daughter* (2008)

THERE WAS ONCE A GIRL WHO WAS BORN TO FIGHT … and to die.

A war raged on the planet Messaline between humans and Hath. Casualties were high and both sides used machines to replenish their forces with battle-ready soldiers. The war raged for generations until nobody could remember what they were fighting for.

On the seventh day of the war, a girl emerged from the machine who was different. She had been grown using a skin sample taken from the Doctor, against his will. This meant she was part Time Lord – the Doctor's daughter.

Her mind was embedded with military history and tactics but she didn't have a name. The Doctor called her a "generated anomaly", at which **Donna** suggested the name Jenny. Jenny approved.

The Doctor tried to keep his distance from this creation. Her soldier programming meant that her natural instinct was to fight the Hath. When they invaded the tunnel, she triggered an explosion to block their path, despite the Hath having captured one of the Doctor's friends, **Martha**. The Doctor abhorred violence, but Jenny thought her father was like a soldier in how he fought back and devised strategies, even if he didn't carry a weapon. Were they really so different?

Jenny was ready to listen to her father, and was persuaded to put down her gun and not kill the malicious Cobb. She had learned that she had a choice, and was keen to follow the Doctor, to travel with him to other worlds.

When the Doctor ended the war between the humans and the Hath, Cobb tried to shoot him. Jenny bravely jumped in the way of the bullet, and then died in the Doctor's arms. He had finally accepted her as his daughter – but she was taken from him.

But then, after he was gone, her Time Lord DNA helped revive her. Inspired by the Doctor, Jenny stole a shuttlecraft and went to explore the universe, save civilisations, defeat creatures and do lots of running, just like her dad.

JENNY FLINT & MADAME VASTRA

PLAYED BY **Catrin Stewart and Neve McIntosh**

OCCUPATION **Consulting detectives**

FIRST APPEARANCE **A Good Man Goes to War** (2011)

LONG AGO, A GIRL LIVED AMONG THE DINOSAURS. When catastrophe threatened her planet, Vastra and the rest of the Silurian people took shelter deep underground and slept for millions of years.

She was rudely awoken in the late 19th century, when apes crashed through her hibernation chamber, killing some of her sisters. Angrily, Vastra tried to avenge them, attacking the stupid apes. But an ape-like alien called the Doctor intervened. He explained that these apes, or "humans", had taken over the Earth in the absence of Vastra's people and established their own civilisation.

Vastra was smart enough to learn to live among them, hiding her lizard face behind a veil. She made herself useful as a consulting detective, helping the police track down notorious criminals, whom she ate. She also made friends among the apes, including one in particular – Jenny Flint.

Cheeky Londoner Jenny was an adept burglar and fighter, who took a job as Vastra's chambermaid, though there was clearly something more between them. She accepted who Vastra was, her eating criminals and her occasional roving eye. They fell deeply in love.

The Doctor had helped Vastra adjust to the ape world, and had saved Jenny's life on the first occasion they met. Jenny and Vastra were keen to repay the debt, so they helped him sneak past the security systems of the asteroid Demon's Run, where they then took on an army.

Skilled in unarmed combat, and fighting with swords or laser guns, Jenny and Vastra made a formidable team. It was their kindness, compassion and love that often aided the Doctor as much as their fighting skills: they comforted **Amy Pond** when her baby was kidnapped, looked after the grieving Doctor when Amy was lost to him, and counselled **Clara Oswald** when she felt conflicting emotions about the Doctor's regeneration. They took in Sontaran nurse Strax when he had nowhere else to go, employing him as a butler and keeping his violent tendencies in check.

The Doctor trusted Vastra implicitly, and she knew him with rare insight. "Give him hell," she instructed Clara. "He'll always need it."

JOAN REDFERN

PLAYED BY **Jessica Hynes**

OCCUPATION **School matron**

FIRST APPEARANCE *Human Nature* (2007)

ONCE, THERE WAS A HEARTBROKEN WOMAN WHO DARED TO LOVE AGAIN.

As a child, playing in secret dens and hideaways, Joan fell for a boy, and grew up to marry him. He died in the Second Boer War and 13 years later, Joan was still angry with the army.

By then, she was matron at Farringham School for Boys. Watching boys being taught to use guns made her furious and sad, as she confided to new master, John Smith. Attracted to him, she showed interest in the strange fairy tale he was writing, in which his alter-ego was really an alien traveller in time. She was jealous of other women in his life – **Rose** in his stories, and **Martha**, the maid at the school who'd known John in the past.

66 *I'm doing my duty, just as much as you.* 99

Joan could be a snob and her perspective was tainted by prejudice. It seemed harder for her to believe that a black woman could qualify as a doctor than that John's wild stories of time travel were true.

But true they were, and the school and nearby village were attacked by an alien family who sought John's alter-ego, the Doctor. He had turned himself into a human to evade them, but it hadn't worked.

Joan kept a cool head in the crisis, helping the boys to escape the invaders. She also saw that the only way to save the village – and the world – was for John to die so that the Doctor could return.

Horribly, she and John then glimpsed the future they might have had together – a long and happy marriage, their loved ones all kept safe. That made their sacrifice all the more extraordinary.

The restored Doctor defeated the aliens. Later, he offered Joan a chance to travel with him in time and space. But the man she loved was dead, and she blamed the Doctor for all that had befallen her village – and for the personal loss from which she would never recover.

JOSEPHINE "JO" GRANT

PLAYED BY **Katy Manning**

OCCUPATION **UNIT agent, explorer, activist**

FIRST APPEARANCE *Terror of the Autons* (1971)

A GIRL ONCE DREAMED OF WORKING IN SECRET INTELLIGENCE, and persuaded her influential uncle to help get her a job at UNIT. Jo soon lost any romantic ideas about her work, later complaining that she spent her hours filing, making tea and generally being a dogsbody. That is, except when she assisted the Doctor.

He was UNIT's scientific advisor, and Jo had not even passed general science at A-level. In fact, the first time she met the Doctor, she wrecked one of his experiments because she'd thought it was on fire. But he couldn't be cross with her for long, especially when she applied herself to her work so diligently.

> " *I'm a fully qualified agent, you know. Cryptology, safe-breaking, explosives.* "

Her eagerness would continue to get her into trouble in their time together, such as when she decided to pursue the evil Master on her own, got captured and hypnotised, and then tried to blow up UNIT HQ. But she also learned from her mistakes and experience, gradually building up a resistance to the Master's mesmeric powers.

It wasn't just villains she resisted, declining the advances of the handsome king of the planet Peladon and the brave Latep, a Thal from the planet Skaro. She did agree to a night on the town with UNIT's Captain Yates, but then got sidetracked by a test flight in the TARDIS.

Jo was devoted to the Doctor, but never quite shared his enthusiasm for the wonders of time and space. When, after several adventures on Earth with him, she finally got a trip in the TARDIS, she wasn't much impressed by her first view of an alien world. "I want to go back to Earth," she said.

On that same trip, she glimpsed Earth's future: over-populated, heavily polluted, not a blade of grass left on the planet and a harsh political regime. Could that future be prevented from happening? She was determined to try.

JO WAS KEEN TO SUPPORT A PROTEST against a chemicals company polluting the Welsh countryside, on Earth in her own time. She'd heard on the news about Professor Clifford Jones, the leader of the protest, and felt sure he was fighting for everything she thought important. "In a funny way," she told the Doctor, "he reminds me of a sort of younger you."

When Jo first met Cliff in person, she almost wrecked one of his experiments – much as she had when first meeting the Doctor. And, just as with the Doctor, Cliff couldn't be cross with Jo for long. In fact, they fell quickly in love.

Jo and Cliff, with the Doctor's help, foiled the evil schemes of the chemicals company. Then Cliff was off to the upper reaches of the Amazon to look for alternative and less polluting food sources. He asked Jo to go with him, and to marry him, too. Jo said yes without hesitation.

> " It's time that the world awoke to the alarm bell of pollution instead of sliding down the slippery slopes of … of … of whatever it is. "

"I only left you because I got married," Jo told the Doctor when she finally saw him again, 40 years later. All that time, she had worried why he'd never come back to see her. The truth was, he said, he could hardly keep up with her. She'd been living in huts, climbing trees, tearing down barricades and doing everything from flying kites on Kilimanjaro to sailing down the Yangtze on a tea chest.

Jo had been fighting to protect the Earth, to safeguard its future. If that meant chaining herself to the railings at the G8 summit or handcuffing herself to Zimbabwe's Prime Minister, so be it.

Jo was still happily married to Cliff, with seven children and twelve grandchildren – and a thirteenth on the way. One grandchild, Finn, joined her on her adventures, and his parents had followed Jo's example too: Finn's father was arrested for protesting at a climate change conference, while Finn's mum was in Japan trying to stop whaling ships.

KATARINA

PLAYED BY **Adrienne Hill**

OCCUPATION **Handmaid**

FIRST APPEARANCE *The Myth Makers* (1965)

THERE WAS ONCE A GIRL WHO WAS FATED TO DIE. Katarina served Cassandra, high priestess of the ancient city of Troy, and was one of the few to listen when Cassandra foresaw catastrophe. As the city fell to its enemies, Katarina made her way to what she thought was a temple. There, a woman called **Vicki** asked for help looking for a missing friend. Despite the danger, Katarina found him, then helped the badly wounded Steven stagger to the temple.

She was not surprised to discover that this temple was bigger on the inside, given that it belonged to a god. But the god insisted he was nothing of the kind, and asked Katarina to call him "Doctor". She settled on "My lord."

" The Priestess Cressida told me all would be well, and I knew ... that I was to die. "

The temple left the Earth and began what Katarina understood to be its journey to the "place of perfection", or afterlife. When a stranger walked into the temple, the trusting Katarina assumed he had come to help the wounded man. The stranger tried to steal the temple, and warned Katarina that they were now on a world overrun by evil beings called Daleks. Katarina and her friends had to leave the temple to avoid capture, and stole another vessel to escape to another world.

"You show me so many strange mysteries," she told the Doctor. "With you I know I'm safe."

Sadly, that didn't prove true. A convicted criminal on this other world hid aboard their spaceship and, once it had taken to the air again, sought control by taking Katarina hostage. Keen to protect her friends, she remembered Cassandra's chilling prophecy. In the struggle, she worked the controls to open the airlock, and Katarina and the convict were blasted to their deaths.

The Doctor hoped she had found her way to the place of perfection, and would always remember her as a daughter of the gods.

KATE STEWART

PLAYED BY **Jemma Redgrave**

OCCUPATION **Chief Scientific Officer at UNIT**

FIRST APPEARANCE *The Power of Three* (2012)

THERE WAS ONCE A WOMAN WHO WAS EXTREMELY RELIABLE.

Kate was head of research at UNIT but her job included giving soldiers orders, even telling them when they could or couldn't shoot someone. Her father had been a brigadier at UNIT – and a good friend of the Doctor's – but Kate did not want any favours because of the connection, preferring to prove herself on merit.

She fought to run UNIT on the basis of science and evidence – a gruelling endeavour, though she was supported by highly talented advisors such as **Petronella Osgood**. But for all Kate wanted to act rationally and logically, she could be impulsive, having the TARDIS moved by helicopter without checking first that the Doctor was inside.

She could be ruthless too, threatening to blow up London to stop an invasion, or shooting a Zygon, five rounds rapid, then coolly taking its place to get into Zygon High Command.

Kate could confidently hold her own against the US president or the Secretary-General of the UN, and in the event of alien invasion was tasked with carrying out protocols agreed by all the world's leaders: namely, forcing the Doctor to co-operate. She also tracked down and vetted the Doctor's various friends and companions to ensure their knowledge of him and the TARDIS could never be used against Earth.

Intelligent, stubborn and with a dry sense of humour, perhaps Kate's greatest quality was her willingness to admit when she was wrong. She was ready to release a poison that would kill the 20 million Zygons living secretly on Earth until she heard the Doctor's impassioned plea. Then she backed down and apologised.

Being in UNIT's Black Archive, where memories were routinely wiped, she'd forgotten that he'd had to persuade her not to do so 15 times previously ... *That's* how reliable she was.

MADAME KOVARIAN

PLAYED BY **Frances Barber**

OCCUPATION **Leader of the Kovarian Chapter**

FIRST APPEARANCE *Day of the Moon* (2011)

THERE WAS ONCE A WOMAN DESPERATE TO STOP A WAR.

Kovarian was brilliant, ruthless and from a time where billions of lives – perhaps even reality itself – were at risk. The Doctor was defending a small community on Trenzalore from aliens ready to reignite the Time War. Kovarian decided to stop this conflict from ever happening.

She broke away from the Church of the Papal Mainframe – which supported the Doctor's efforts – and travelled back in time with "confessional priests" called Silents who were genetically engineered so people forgot them the moment they looked away. To remember them, Kovarian wore a distinctive eye-drive, like an eye-patch over one eye.

Her plan was to eradicate the Doctor at an earlier point in his timeline, before he ever reached Trenzalore. First, her Silents destroyed the TARDIS, and almost destroyed the universe. The Doctor repaired the damage but cracks were left across space and time, including the one on Trenzalore that started the battle there.

Next, Kovarian kidnapped the Doctor's pregnant companion, **Amy Pond**, and replaced her with a duplicate so the Doctor wouldn't notice. The baby was born on the asteroid Demon's Run, where Kovarian was defended by an army. The Doctor attacked with his own army – including **Madame Vastra** – and rescued his friends.

Except Kovarian delighted in revealing that she had switched the real baby for a duplicate. She escaped, and as the baby grew, Kovarian engineered her to become a psychopath who would grow up to kill the Doctor. In fact, the grown-up baby – **River Song** – helped save the Doctor's life. He later said he wouldn't have reached Trenzalore without her. Kovarian's schemes to *stop* the conflict actually helped create it.

The ungrateful Silents turned on Kovarian anyway. Amy, taking revenge for the loss of her baby, left Kovarian to die … Except that this was in an aborted timeline, in a world that never was. Perhaps Kovarian survived …

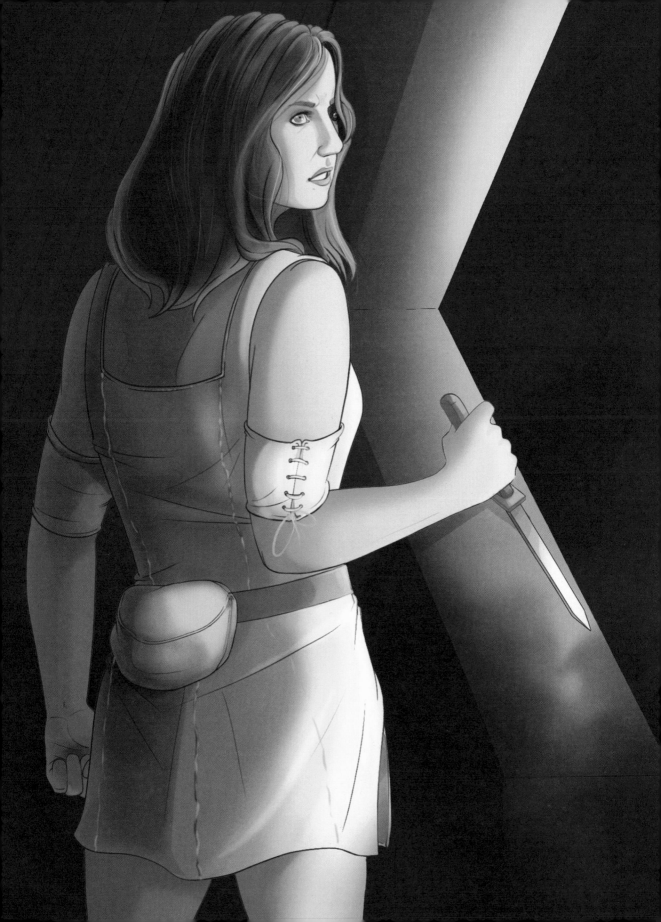

LEELA

PLAYED BY **Louise Jameson**

OCCUPATION **Warrior of the Sevateem**

FIRST APPEARANCE *The Face of Evil* (1977)

THERE WAS ONCE A YOUNG WOMAN WHO GREW UP ON A HOSTILE WORLD.

Leela was curious and intelligent – for all she lacked formal education – and she openly dared to question whether her tribe's god, Xoanon, really existed. For this, she faced terrible punishment. Her father, Sole, volunteered to take her place and was killed. Leela was banished, and alone in the wilds of the planet she met her tribe's greatest enemy, the Evil One himself!

Except the Evil One claimed to be a traveller called the Doctor. Bravely, Leela helped him uncover the truth about Xoanon: he was really a mis-programmed computer that had imposed these harsh conditions on Leela's people, who were actually the descendants of a planetary survey team from Earth. Xoanon was breeding them to be independent, strong and bold.

With Leela's help, the Doctor fixed the mad computer and set Leela's people free. She then boldly forced her way into his TARDIS and joined him on his adventures.

Her savage skills were often helpful in pursuing or fighting adversaries, and even identifying a murderer's method just from the sound of the victim's scream. Her instincts and perhaps some low-level telepathy helped warn of impending danger. But she also asked intelligent questions and was eager to learn. Brought up to believe in magic, she now thought it better to believe in science.

Leela was the first companion the Doctor voluntarily took to his own planet, Gallifrey, just as it was being invaded by both the Vardans and the Sontarans. For all their technical brilliance, the Time Lords needed her to teach them how to survive and to fight back.

During this conflict, Leela met and fell in love with the commander of the Time Lords' chancellery guard. She decided to stay on Gallifrey with him. The Doctor missed her wedding, but on his next visit was glad to hear she was well and happy.

LOCUSTA

PLAYED BY **Anne Tirard**

OCCUPATION **Official poisoner**

FIRST APPEARANCE *The Romans* (1965)

THERE WAS ONCE A WOMAN WHOSE LIFE DEPENDED ON DEATH. It was her job – her *vocation* – to make poisons for the highest persons in the Roman court.

In Ancient Rome, poison was an accepted tool for bringing about political change. In AD 54, Agrippina – wife of the emperor Claudius – wanted her husband out of the way so she might install her son, Nero, as ruler of the empire. It was said that Agrippina consulted Locusta the Gaul, a woman who made poisons that made it look like her clients' rivals and rich relations had died of natural causes. Locusta had been caught and sentenced to death, but Agrippina promised to free her in return for a means of killing the emperor. However, once Claudius was dead the treacherous Agrippina blamed Locusta for what had happened, and Locusta was locked up.

A year later, Emperor Nero offered Locusta her freedom in exchange for a poison to kill his teenage half-brother Britannicus. When she merely made him sick, Nero was said to have beaten her with his own hands. Locusta, who had been trying to ensure that Nero wasn't held responsible, tried again and this time Britannicus died. Now Nero rewarded her handsomely.

In AD 64, the Doctor visited the court of the Emperor Nero, where Locusta had a workshop and was kept busy making poisons for the family. She didn't know who the poisons would be given to, and didn't see why anyone should blame her for the deaths either. They would understand; she was only doing her job.

Nero's wife Poppaea asked Locusta for a poison to kill one of Nero's new slaves – a woman called **Barbara Wright** who Poppaea believed had ambitions to be empress. Locusta supplied the poison, but **Vicki** switched the goblets. Furious at this failure, Poppaea had Locusta sent to her death in the arena.

However, historians of the time suggest Locusta was reprieved, if only for a few years. Then, when Nero was dead, many of those associated with his tyrannical regime – including Locusta – were paraded through the streets of Rome in chains before being executed.

LUCY SAXON

PLAYED BY **Alexandra Moen**

OCCUPATION **The Master's wife, Britain's First Lady**

FIRST APPEARANCE *The Sound of Drums* (2007)

THERE WAS ONCE A YOUNG WOMAN WHO MADE A CHOICE.

Lucy came from a good family, who sent her to the respected Roedean School – though, as she admitted herself, she was not especially bright. A journalist described Lucy as "essentially harmless", missing her cold ambition.

A man called Harry charmed Lucy and took her to the stars, trillions of years in the future, where she saw the last remnants of humanity, and the whole of creation coming apart. It made her realise there was no point to anything.

Back in her own time, Lucy chose to become Harry's wife. Eighteen months later, she was at his side as he became Prime Minister. She knew her husband planned to open the way for a full-scale invasion of Earth by the Toclafane – in truth, the remnants of humanity she had met in the distant future – but still she stood by him, even when he murdered the US President, imprisoned his enemy the Doctor, and unleashed the Toclafane on the world.

But a year later, their relationship had dramatically changed. Her husband now dictated what she wore. He taunted her by showing interest in other women, and promising to take them to the stars. He hit her.

So Lucy made her choice. When the people of Earth used a telepathic field called the Archangel Network to free and empower the Doctor, she joined them. When it looked like the Master might accept perpetual imprisonment for his terrible crimes, she didn't think it was enough, so she shot her husband.

Thanks to the Doctor's TARDIS, all that her husband had done was reversed. But Lucy was one of those who remembered the events of that terrible year. Some plotted to resurrect her husband, using "potions of life" and his biometrical signature, but Lucy had already planned for this and, through family contacts, developed a mixture that would counter their efforts.

In the moment of his resurrection, the Master tried to order her to obey him once more, but Lucy had long since made her choice. Defiantly, she threw the mixture at her husband – and seems to have died in the ensuing explosion.

LYNDA MOSS

PLAYED BY **Jo Joyner**

OCCUPATION **Reality TV contestant**

FIRST APPEARANCE *Bad Wolf* (2005)

THERE WAS ONCE A YOUNG WOMAN WHO HAD NO CHOICE.

The Earth that Lynda knew was a polluted, congested place. People hid themselves indoors, watching the 10,000 channels of TV game shows beamed down from the orbiting Game Station. The game shows were all similarly brutal, and contestants had no choice but to take part; like Lynda, they were chosen at random and brought by transmat beam up to the Game Station. To lose, more often than not, meant death.

Lynda was put into one of the 60 games of *Big Brother*, and tried to make the best of it. She was an enthusiastic contestant, supporting other housemates, even when they stole her soap. She hoped the viewers at home would like her and not send her to her doom.

When a strange man suddenly stumbled out of a cupboard, Lynda exclaimed that it was brilliant. This Doctor was determined to escape, and Lynda dared to go with him when he broke out. She said she just wanted to get home, but when the Doctor told her he wandered the stars, she hesitantly asked if she might travel with him. "Maybe you could," he said.

They got on well, laughing and joking as they explored. Lynda also got on with the Doctor's friend Captain Jack.

When the Doctor discovered the Game Station was about to be overrun by Daleks, Lynda gamely volunteered to help Jack defend the station. She couldn't fight, but she worked from the Observation Deck, relaying to Jack what the Daleks were doing. With mounting horror, she watched the Daleks descend to the lower decks to exterminate the defenceless people cowering there, and then bomb the continents of Earth.

The Daleks found her, and began burning through the reinforced door. "You know what they say about Earth workmanship," she joked, trying to stay upbeat to the very last. But more Daleks broke through the windows and poor Lynda was exterminated.

MARTHA JONES

PLAYED BY **Freema Agyeman**

OCCUPATION **Doctor, UNIT officer**

FIRST APPEARANCE *Smith and Jones* (2007)

THERE WAS ONCE A YOUNG WOMAN whose brilliance and hard work went unappreciated. Martha was born into a lively family. Martha's parents were divorced and her family argued a lot. She was the peacemaker of her family.

Martha was studying medicine where she encountered a strange patient at Royal Hope Hospital called John Smith. When she examined him, she was stunned to find he had two hearts. Later that day, the hospital was transported to the Moon by alien troops trying to capture a wanted Plasmavore criminal. Even though all inside were fast running out of oxygen, Martha didn't panic like everyone else. When John Smith revealed himself to be an alien called the Doctor, Martha helped him track down that Plasmavore and ensured justice was done. Impressed with Martha's bravery and performance under pressure, the Doctor invited her to travel through time and space in the TARDIS.

> ❝ I spent a lot of time with you thinking I was second best. But you know what? I am good. ❞

On her many trips with the Doctor, Martha's professional skills and manner proved useful. She was very accepting of other alien species and treated them equally, even tending to their wounds.

Martha developed a crush on the Doctor but he never noticed her advances, which gradually ate away at her over the course of their time together. It was especially hard for her when he was disguised as a human schoolteacher and she had to look after him – and watch as he fell in love with someone else.

She stepped up from medical student to rebel activist when the Doctor was captured by the Master. Martha travelled the world for a year, telling the story of her friend to inspire people during the Master's rule over the planet, which generated enough psychic energy to release him.

WHILE SHE'D HAD AN INCREDIBLE TIME with the Doctor, Martha wanted to become a doctor herself and look after people on Earth. She didn't want to waste years of her life pining after the unattainable Time Lord, and so she chose to end her travels with him.

As a qualified doctor, Martha joined UNIT to help protect the Earth from alien menaces. She was ready to call the Doctor back to Earth when his expertise was needed. When the Doctor seemed unhappy that she now worked with soldiers, Martha snapped back that, "If anyone got me used to fighting, it's you." Besides, she was determined to exert her influence and make UNIT a better organisation.

> ## " I've got to work from the inside, and by staying inside, maybe I stand a chance of making them better. "

Having helped to defeat an invasion by the Sontarans, Martha then took one more trip in the TARDIS, to the planet Messaline. But she stood by her decision *not* to travel with the Doctor, and was keen to return home to her life and job and fiancé.

A year later, when the Earth was transported to the Medusa Cascade and invaded by Daleks, Martha accepted her terrifying responsibility as a UNIT officer and attempted to activate the Osterhagen Project to destroy the Earth, rather than let it be used by the Daleks to create a Reality Bomb. Although the Daleks stopped her using the key, Martha teamed up with the Doctor and several of his companions to defeat the Daleks. She and the gang then all piloted the TARDIS so that it could bring Earth back to its proper place in the universe.

Martha eventually married Mickey Smith, a young man and former boyfriend of **Rose Tyler** who had also travelled with the Doctor. Happy, fulfilled and appreciated, Martha continued to defend the Earth.

MELANIE BUSH

PLAYED BY **Bonnie Langford**

OCCUPATION **Computer programmer**

FIRST APPEARANCE *The Trial of a Time Lord* (1986)

THERE WAS ONCE A YOUNG WOMAN WHO WANTED A MORE EXCITING LIFE.
Mel was a computer programmer, living quietly in the Sussex village of
Pease Pottage. Then she met the Doctor and embraced his life of adventures.
Travelling with him, she was always ready to answer mayday calls, investigate
murders and battle villains.

She was keen to help in any way she could, even cajoling the Doctor into
losing weight by installing an exercise bike in the TARDIS and making him drink
carrot juice. However, Mel's eagerness could land her in trouble, as could her
trusting nature: she once accepted an invitation to take tea and biscuits with a
pair of old ladies who really wanted to eat her! She could also ruin the Doctor's
ingenious schemes by not realising what he was up to and rushing in to help.

" *Well, calm down. Let's apply a bit of logic, shall we?* "

It was true that she could be a bit of a goody-goody, automatically tidying a
messy bedroom or suggesting a game of I-Spy to kill some time – both of which
failed to impress the more openly rebellious **Ace**. But for all Ace might call Mel
"Doughnut", the two quickly became good friends. Ace encouraged Mel's wilder
side. Together they explored the lower depths of Iceworld when the Doctor had
told them not to, and Mel even set off explosives.

It was Mel who prompted the Doctor to invite Ace to join him in the TARDIS.
She had decided it was time to leave, but not to go back to her safe, quiet home.
She still wanted to explore the stars, so invited herself on board a spaceship,
the *Nosferatu II*, captained by Sabalom Glitz. Others might have balked at the
thought of signing up with such a character, who had previously sold all his crew.
But, as ever, Mel went ahead eagerly, wanting to ensure he made no further
dodgy deals. She always saw – and always brought out – the best in everyone.

MERCY HARTIGAN

PLAYED BY **Dervla Kerwin**

OCCUPATION **Matron of St Joseph's Workhouse**

FIRST APPEARANCE *The Next Doctor* (2009)

THERE WAS ONCE A WOMAN WHO LONGED TO BE SET FREE.

Until December 1851, Mercy Hartigan was the hard-working matron at St Joseph's Workhouse. London's workhouses offered accommodation and work to the poor in the days before welfare and benefits. While the wealthy men of the city looked on, smiling, at what they saw as the fruits of their generous charity, Mercy was left to scrub the children's filthy beds. She grew to hate those men.

Then she met Cybermen who'd fallen through time from a howling wilderness called the Void. They offered Mercy a bargain – her liberation in exchange for help in assembling a workforce to build a giant CyberKing. This dreadnought class ship would then be the frontline of a full invasion, with a Cyberfactory in its chest, ready to convert millions.

Ingenious as well as ambitious, Mercy soon ordered the Cybermen to kill a keen advocate of children's charities. His funeral was attended by the respectable men who ran the city's workhouses. Mercy had them all kidnapped and Cyber-converted, so that they then surrendered the children in their care to work for the Cybermen. Ironically, given her first name, she gave instructions for all others at the funeral to be killed.

Her bargain with the Cybermen gave her confidence to say and do things no ordinary woman of the time would ever dare to. But she had no say at all when the Cybermen decided to use her living mind to run the CyberKing systems. Regardless, she broke the grip of Cyber control and forced the Cybermen to obey *her*, bringing to their cold logic and strength her own imagination, fury and passion as the CyberKing crushed London underfoot.

Awed by Mercy's incredible mental strength, the Doctor wanted to free her, but when she refused he was left with no choice. To save humanity from conquest and conversion, he broke the connection between Mercy and the Cybermen, confronting her with the truth of what she had become.

Horrified by all she had done, Mercy destroyed herself, and the Cybermen with her.

MISSY

PLAYED BY **Michelle Gomez**

OCCUPATION **The Master**

FIRST APPEARANCE *Deep Breath* (2014)

THERE ONCE LIVED A WOMAN WHO DELIGHTED IN CRUELTY. Any situation she wandered into, she would only make worse. She killed for the thrill of it, loving how people popped like balloons.

She would kill randomly, just for fun. And she would devise outlandish schemes to create maximum havoc. She manoeuvred **Clara Oswald** into meeting the Doctor, knowing the two of them might end up becoming the "Hybrid" of Time Lord legend, prophesied to unravel the web of time.

Missy founded the 3W Institute, uploading the minds of Earth's dead to the Nethersphere and then converting them into a huge army of Cybermen. She didn't want this army for herself; she presented it as a gift to the Doctor, hoping to corrupt him into becoming a dictator. She gleefully murdered his friend **Petronella Osgood** among other terrible acts, all to provoke him.

To the Doctor's horror, Missy insisted that she and he were very similar. She said all the things she had done were because she wanted her friend back, revealing that she was a female incarnation of his old enemy the Master, who he'd known since childhood. She'd taken her new name from Mistress, the female form of Master.

Given the atrocities she'd committed, the Doctor seemed ready to take drastic action, breaching his own moral code to shoot her in cold blood. But the decision was taken out of his hands by a Cyberman, and Missy escaped.

As his oldest surviving friend, she was then given the Doctor's last will and testament in the form of a confession dial. Curious as to why the Doctor thought he was dying, Missy threatened the world just to get Clara's attention, and then the two of them traced the Doctor to a particular moment in history. But the alliance did not last long: on the planet Skaro, Missy trapped Clara inside a Dalek casing and then tried to convince the Doctor to shoot her.

SOME TIME LATER, MISSY WAS CAPTURED and sentenced to death for the crimes committed over her many lifetimes, and the Doctor was invited to carry out the sentence. Despite their differences, he sabotaged the execution and locked her inside a Quantum Fold Chamber. The Doctor believed that over time, he would be able to rehabilitate her. He kept her imprisoned in a vault at St Luke's university. Over the long years, Missy came to see her wrongdoing, and even cried for the people she had killed. But had she really changed?

Missy was released from the Vault occasionally under strict supervision. With the Doctor keen to test her conversion, he let her lead an expedition to a colony ship from Mondas with his companions, **Bill** and Nardole. There, she bumped into her previous incarnation, the Master, and she joined forces with him. But when the Cybermen turned on the Doctor, she whacked the Master over the head and saved the Doctor's life, saying she had been on his side all along.

> ❝ *I don't even know why I'm crying. Why? Why do I keep doing that now?* ❞

Yet Missy remained torn. When it seemed there was no hope of saving the people on board the ship from the gathering army of Cybermen, the Master ignored the Doctor's appeal to make a stand anyway, and Missy left with him. Then she changed her mind and wanted to go back to the Doctor. When the Master would not agree, she fatally wounded him, knowing he'd regenerate into her and then see things differently.

But being with her past self affected her memories, so she had forgotten what then happened next: the dying Master shot her, with a full blast from his laser screwdriver that would, he thought, prevent her regenerating again.

As he hurried off to his TARDIS and to become the woman she had been, Missy could see the darkly comic side of all this. With cruel irony, she *had* changed, but the Doctor would never know.

QUEEN NEFERTITI

PLAYED BY **Riann Steele**

OCCUPATION **Queen of Egypt**

FIRST APPEARANCE *Dinosaurs on a Spaceship* (2011)

LADY OF GRACE, Sweet of Love, Lady of All Women and Lady of the Two Lands, Nefertiti had many titles as queen of Egypt and wife of the great pharaoh, Amonhotep IV. They had six daughters, but Nefertiti thought her husband boring, "the male equivalent of a sleeping potion."

In 1334 BC, the country was attacked by weapon-bearing giant alien locusts. Nefertiti and a traveller known as the Doctor brilliantly stopped the invasion. The Doctor told Nefertiti that her people would need her leadership and reassurance after such an ordeal, but she was determined to join him on more extraordinary adventures. He couldn't resist her wiles, and she seems to have been the earliest-born Earth person ever to travel in his TARDIS.

In AD 2367, Nefertiti was part of a perilous mission to prevent a strange spaceship from colliding with Earth. She took the advances in technology in her stride, asking the staff of the Indian Space Agency if they had been able to communicate with this craft, an ability far beyond her own time. She also took it in her stride when the spaceship turned out to be full of creatures called dinosaurs.

Nefertiti held her own against the people of the future, too. When Riddell, a hunter from AD 1902, said he didn't take orders from women, she commanded him, "Then learn." When he made further sexist comments, she told him she would snap his neck in a heartbeat. But in fact, she was drawn to this man of action, so unlike her tedious husband.

When a wicked trader called Solomon realised who Nefertiti was, and how valuable a queen of Ancient Egypt might be, she coolly volunteered herself as his prisoner to save the lives of her friends. But she would never be his possession, and when the chance came she curtly knocked him down. In so doing, she helped the Doctor save the spaceship and the dinosaurs onboard.

Nefertiti then settled with Riddell in the African plains in 1902. A strong ruler can do anything she chooses.

NYSSA

PLAYED BY **Sarah Sutton**

OCCUPATION **Bioengineer, expert in cybernetics**

FIRST APPEARANCE *The Keeper of Traken* (1981)

THERE WAS ONCE A YOUNG WOMAN who longed to make the most of her skills.

Growing up on the planet Traken, Nyssa was encouraged by her father – a consul and determined scientist – to study bioengineering and cybernetics. She became highly skilled in both.

When her father remarried, it was decided that Nyssa should take over her new stepmother's job of tending the Melkur, an evil creature frozen in stone long ago who ultimately proved to be the Master. She obeyed her father without complaint, but showed her more spirited side when working with the Doctor to thwart the Master's diabolical plans.

Soon after the Doctor left Traken, Nyssa's beloved father disappeared. To find him, she journeyed to meet the Doctor on the planet Logopolis. There Nyssa discovered the Master had murdered her father and taken over his body. His first actions in this stolen body were to shut down the systems on Logopolis and unleash an entropy wave to consume the universe. Nyssa had already lost her father. Now her home planet and star system were lost, too. In stopping the entropy wave, the Doctor was killed too, but transformed into a new man.

Nyssa continued to travel with this younger version of the Doctor. He relied on her technical skills and ability to recognise items of advanced technology. Her logical reasoning even helped her make sense of the TARDIS controls. But for all this serious scientific knowledge, Nyssa had a keen sense of fun. When she met Ann Talbot, a young woman who looked just like her, they confused their friends by swapping places. She embraced opportunities to learn a new dance or to try new food, and generally enjoyed every moment of her time on the TARDIS.

But Nyssa was keen to put her scientific knowledge to the service of others. After contracting Lazars disease on the space station Terminus and surviving its hit-or-miss cure, she stayed behind to help to turn it into a proper hospital.

OHILA

PLAYED BY **Clare Higgins**

OCCUPATION **High Priestess**

FIRST APPEARANCE *The Night of the Doctor* (2013)

ONCE UPON A TIME, THERE WAS A WOMAN WHO COULDN'T DIE.

As the High Priestess of the Sisterhood of Karn, Ohila was custodian of the Elixir of Life, which made her and her followers immortal. The all-female sisterhood devoted themselves to the Sacred Flame, which produced the elixir. But their age, wisdom and psychic powers also gave them tremendous influence over others, including their neighbours – the Time Lords.

When, during the Last Great Time War, the Eighth Doctor crash landed on Karn, wise Ohila decided that he was the only hope for peace. She persuaded him to drink a modified version of the Elixir of Life, which would transform him from Doctor to Soldier. The War Doctor was born.

> " *At the end of everything, you must expect the company of immortals.* "

Long after the Time War, Ohila had grown to respect and even advise the Doctor, considering him a friend. The Doctor trusted Ohila and gave her his confession dial – his last will and testament – which she passed on to **Missy**.

After the Doctor was trapped in his confession dial for 4.5 billion years, Ohila joined him on his home planet of Gallifrey, where she held her own with the High Council. She was amused by the attempts of legendary Time Lord President Rassilon to communicate with the Doctor, telling him that the Doctor blamed him for the horrors of the Time War.

For all she enjoyed watching Rassilon squirm, she was also worried by the Doctor's actions in saving **Clara Oswald** from the moment of her death. She thought he was being irrational, and grew increasingly furious; he was going too far, and going against all he believed in by breaking the laws of time so brazenly. He ignored her warnings, but would soon discover that this wise and ancient woman was, as ever, quite right.

PERPUGILLIAM "PERI" BROWN

PLAYED BY **Nicola Bryant**

OCCUPATION **Botany student**

FIRST APPEARANCE *Planet of Fire* (1984)

THERE WAS ONCE A YOUNG WOMAN WHO LONGED TO TRAVEL.

Peri was a botany student in her native United States, but in the summer break she travelled with her mother and stepfather to Lanzarote. There she could help with her stepfather's archaeological work or go on trips with her mother, but Peri was soon bored.

Impulsively, she cashed in her ticket back home and used the money to pay for a trip to Morocco with some English "guys" she'd just met. Her stepfather objected, but when she wouldn't listen, he stranded her on a boat so that she'd miss her flight. Refusing to let him win, Peri tried to swim ashore, but ran into difficulties. A young man rescued her and took her to recover inside a strange police box, which was really a spaceship. Soon Peri found herself on an alien world.

The owner of the police box, the Doctor, was happy to take Peri back to Earth, but she told him how much she wanted to travel, and he welcomed her aboard. They were soon caught up in a dangerous adventure on Androzani Minor. To save Peri from a deadly poison, the Doctor sacrificed his own life – and then, to her amazement, he changed.

Whereas the man she had known had been polite and sweet, the new Doctor was abrasive and unstable. But Peri had always been headstrong, and would not be pushed around. For all they argued, they were also good friends.

Peri made some effort to keep up with her studies, collecting flowers from the worlds she visited, saying she would take them with her when she went back to college. She learned to work many of the TARDIS systems, and would often check the readings before stepping outside anywhere new.

She made friends quickly on the worlds they visited, especially with rebels and freedom fighters. That included Yrcanos, warrior King of Krontep. Just as with the Doctor, Peri easily held her own against this brash, impulsive figure. And something more developed between them. Separated from the Doctor, she became Yrcanos's warrior queen.

PETRONELLA OSGOOD(S)

PLAYED BY **Ingrid Oliver**

OCCUPATION **Scientist**

FIRST APPEARANCE *The Day of the Doctor* (2013)

THERE WAS ONCE A GIRL WHO WAS DETERMINED TO DO HER BEST.

Osgood had horrible memories of her childhood. She was jealous of her pretty sister, and wracked with self-doubt. Her asthma played up whenever she got excited, so she was permanently reaching for her inhaler.

But Osgood had a brilliant mind and proved herself as a scientist. She was snapped up by UNIT, working directly under Chief Scientific Officer **Kate Stewart**. In learning UNIT's secrets, Osgood was inspired by the Doctor's work there in the 1970s. She was soon a dedicated fan, even often dressing in similar clothes.

> ❝ *Goodness, you're not actually dead. Oh, that's tremendous news.* ❞

One day, she got the chance to meet her hero when UNIT brought him to the National Gallery to investigate a strange painting. The Doctor sent Osgood and her colleague to investigate some dust in the Under-Gallery. She cleverly worked out that the dust was in fact the remains of statues that had been smashed by shapeshifting Zygons – who were hiding in the room with them. Osgood was cornered by one of the Zygons, which took her form and taunted her. But Osgood tripped up the Zygon, who was standing on her scarf, grabbed back her inhaler, and escaped.

Osgood bravely rescued Kate, who had also been duplicated, and followed her to UNIT's Black Archive to confront the Zygons. Neither side trusted the other, and the world's future was in great jeopardy – until three incarnations of the Doctor showed up just in time and wiped everyone's memory so nobody could remember who was the original human and who the Zygon duplicate. They were equals.

Except the clever Osgoods quickly worked out which of them was which; the need for an inhaler gave it away. But to aid the Doctor's plan and preserve peace between the two species, they kept their knowledge secret. In fact, the peace would now depend on the two of them ...

OSGOOD AND OSGOOD CREATED OPERATION DOUBLE, which allowed 20 million Zygons to live peaceably – and invisibly – on Earth, taking the form of other humans. To ensure the Zygons didn't cause the humans harm, the Doctor gave the two Osgoods a special box. Press the button inside and it would unmask every Zygon, presenting them in their real form and provoking a war. This device was known by UNIT and by the Zygons as the "Osgood box", partly because she looked after it, and partly because the two Osgoods were so crucial to keeping the peace.

In the meantime, the Osgoods continued with their work for UNIT, assisting the Doctor against a Cyberman invasion – until one of them was cruelly murdered by **Missy**, as part of a plan to provoke the Doctor into taking charge of the Cyberman army. A plan that failed.

> ❝ What's today? Oh, you know, same old, same old. Defending the Earth. ❞

The remaining Osgood would not reveal if she was the human original or Zygon duplicate, hoping that this would help maintain the peace between the two species. She was working in Turmezistan during the Zygon uprising, where she was captured by the aliens. The Doctor helped her escape, but she refused to tell even him if she were human or Zygon. She and her late "sister" had been the living embodiment of the peace, and she would give all the lives that she had to protect it.

Together, the Doctor and this Osgood survived attempts on their lives by a renegade Zygon faction who wanted to start a war with humanity. Osgood cleverly realised that Bonnie, the renegade Zygon who attacked them, had taken **Clara Oswald**'s form, and so was being influenced by the real Clara's memories and feelings.

Inspired by this, the Doctor was able to convince Bonnie to stand down, referring to arguments that the real Clara had once made to him. Bonnie then decided to take on Osgood's form so there were two of them once more. Together, they protected planet Earth from alien threats.

POLLY

PLAYED BY **Anneke Wills**

OCCUPATION **Secretary**

FIRST APPEARANCE *The War Machines* (1966)

THERE WAS ONCE A YOUNG WOMAN WHO WANTED TO HELP.

Polly had a good job as a well-respected secretary. In her free time, she made the most of swinging London, visiting fashionable shops in Carnaby Street and going to trendy nightclubs. One thing she *didn't* like was her boss's new supercomputer, which could type faster than she could, "and it never makes mistakes, wretched thing." Her instincts were spot on: soon the computer was trying to enslave humanity.

Polly helped the Doctor battle the computer. She and her new friend Ben Jackson then stumbled into the TARDIS just as the Doctor had set it in flight, so beginning a whirlwind of exciting adventures.

> " *Any time you want a bit of brightness in your life, come to Pol'.* "

Polly was always resourceful wherever they landed. She escaped a jail cell in 17th-century Cornwall by playing on local superstition. She came up with a chemical mixture, based on nail-polish remover, to fight Cybermen on the Moon. And she encouraged other women, such as the Highlander Kirsty, to be more outgoing and independent. Together they dared to capture a young lieutenant in the English Army. Soon the lieutenant was working with Polly to expose a wicked slave trader and bring him to justice.

For all she was plucky, Polly would admit to being scared by the monstrous things she encountered. All the same, she did her best to help any way she could, even if that was just making coffee for people and offering soothing words.

Ben teased her for her manners and being a bit posh, but she seemed to enjoy him calling her "Duchess". When the TARDIS brought them back to London on the same day they had left, the Doctor could see they were both keen to stay. The two of them hurried off together to begin a new life, and were last heard of running an orphanage in India.

THE RANI

PLAYED BY **Kate O'Mara**

OCCUPATION **Neurochemist, Time Lady**

FIRST APPEARANCE *The Mark of the Rani* (1985)

ONCE UPON A TIME, a young chemistry student conducted an experiment on some mice. The mice turned into monsters and ate a cat, one belonging to the president of that distant world. The disgraced student was sent away into exile. Her people had simply not appreciated her genius!

Centuries later, the former student ruled the planet Miasimia Goria and now called herself the Rani – from the Sanskrit word meaning 'queen'. She continued with her experiments, but discovered that heightening the awareness of the native population also lowered their ability to sleep. They became difficult for her to control, resulting in mayhem.

The Rani's solution was brilliantly simple: she'd acquire a sleep-inducing chemical from the brains of another species: the humans of the planet Earth. She didn't care that this would make the sleep-deprived humans violent. As she put it on another occasion, "Am I expected to abandon my research because of the side effects on inferior species?"

She *did* care about getting caught by her own people, and so was also careful to visit Earth in times of violence, so that the effects of her work were less likely to be noticed. When this brilliant scheme was sabotaged by the Doctor – an annoying man she'd known on her home planet – the Rani came up with another. She conquered the unassuming inhabitants of the planet Lakertya, then kidnapped geniuses from all through time and space (including the Doctor) to create a giant brain. She planned to use this to calculate a means to turn the planet into a time manipulator, allowing her to rewrite all of history in a cleaner, more logical way.

Again, she didn't care that her clever project would kill everyone on the planet – the native Lakertyans and even the monstrous Tetraps that the Rani had brought with her to police them. However, the Tetraps weren't best pleased to learn that she was going to sacrifice them, and that was her undoing. When the Doctor once again thwarted her schemes, the Tetraps made the Rani *their* slave.

"REINETTE", JEANNE ANTOINETTE POISSON, MARQUISE DE POMPADOUR

PLAYED BY **Sophia Myles**

OCCUPATION **Member of the court of Louis XV**

FIRST APPEARANCE *The Girl in the Fireplace* (2006)

THERE WAS ONCE A GIRL SO CLEVER AND ELEGANT that everyone called her "Reinette", meaning "little Queen." One night, the Doctor stepped out of the fireplace in young Reinette's bedroom and asked if she knew the year. Of course she did: it was 1727. He thanked her and was gone. Months later, the man wandered back into her bedroom and found a scary clockwork robot hiding under her bed!

Years passed and Reinette came to consider those encounters as nothing more than dreams. She remained clever and talented, but became bold and independent. When the Doctor returned to her room – the fireplace was in fact a time window, connected to outer space – reason told Reinette that he could not be real. But she kissed him anyway.

She was also growing ambitious, plotting to meet and amaze the King of France so as to gain power and position. Then the Doctor – and the clockwork robots – returned! The robots said that they and Reinette were "the same". When the Doctor looked into Reinette's mind to see what made her special, Reinette's mental acuity allowed her to look back and know him too.

The robots maintained a 51st-century spaceship, *SS Madame de Pompadour*, which was 37 years old. When the ship became damaged, the malfunctioning robots attempted to fix the systems with organic replacements. They'd been watching their ship's namesake, Reinette, so that when she turned 37 they could take her brain to replace the ship's computer.

The Doctor was ready to strand himself with Reinette to save her life. But without him knowing, Reinette had restored the original fireplace, allowing passage back to the spacecraft. The Doctor told her to pack and come with him, but when he returned seconds later, seven years had passed in Reinette's time, and she had died, tragically, at not quite 43. She left him a farewell letter, which he kept close. She had not only got into his mind, but into his hearts.

RITA

PLAYED BY **Amara Karan**

OCCUPATION **Medical student**

FIRST APPEARANCE *The God Complex* (2011)

THERE WAS ONCE A YOUNG WOMAN WHO WANTED TO DO WELL.

Rita's greatest fear was disappointing her father. She applied herself, working hard as a medical student, and at life generally.

Then, one day when Rita was just starting her shift at the hospital, she must have passed out. She woke up to find herself in a strange hotel. There were other people with her – including an alien – who didn't know how they'd got there, either. And each bedroom of the hotel contained a different nightmare.

Always practical, Rita quickly organised the others. It wasn't that she was any less scared than they were, but she was able to prioritise. For example, she could ignore the fact that one of them was an alien; that was something to freak out about later. When one of the group started getting weird and dangerous, Rita helped to tie him up.

After two days in the hotel, things were getting desperate. But the Doctor and his friends arrived, and Rita and the Doctor hit it off. He seemed just as smart, observant and witty as she was, and keen to put others at ease. She made everyone tea, explaining that this was how, being British, she coped with trauma. "That and tutting," she said.

She also dared to share with the Doctor her theory about where they were. "This is Jahannam," she said – according to the Muslim faith, the part of the afterlife where evildoers are punished. Rita's faith was important to her, and the Doctor thought it might keep her safe from whatever scary creature was preying on people in the hotel. Sadly, he'd got it wrong; the creature scared people so they'd fall back on their faith, which it would then consume. Now it preyed on Rita.

When she realised she was next on the menu, Rita nobly went to face the creature, but asked that the Doctor didn't watch as her faith was stripped from her in the moment before her death. She retained her dignity, her essential self, to the end.

PROFESSOR RIVER SONG

PLAYED BY **Alex Kingston**

OCCUPATION **Archaeologist, criminal**

FIRST APPEARANCE *Silence in the Library* (2008)

ONCE UPON A TIME, a woman knew the Doctor's secrets – even his real name. He was utterly taken aback by this, having never met her before. Just as he started to accept that, in his future, they would become very close, this extraordinary woman gave up her life to save him and all that was to come … Who was she?

Once upon *another* time, a baby girl with awesome powers was stolen from her parents. On the asteroid Demon's Run, **Amy Pond** named her baby Melody, after a childhood friend. She didn't know that, because Melody had been conceived in the TARDIS while it was travelling through the vortex, the child was imbued with abilities like the Time Lords …

" Hello, Sweetie! "

Kovarian stole baby Melody to exploit these powers, bringing up the child in an orphanage in Florida in the 1960s, conditioning her to want to kill the Doctor. But brave Melody was already starting to rebel against her captors, calling for help from the highest authority she could find – the President of the United States – and then escaping.

After six months on the run, she was sick and dying. But she regenerated, becoming a toddler, as if to start her childhood again. She began to search for her parents.

It took about 25 years to track them down, to the village of Leadworth in the UK. Melody slowed her ageing so that she appeared to be eight, the same age as her future parents when she found them. She didn't say who she was – how would they ever believe her? – but they became best friends.

Young Amy told Mels all about the strange, raggedy Doctor she had met. Mels was very taken by these stories, dreaming of the Doctor and sure she'd grow up to marry him. But she was still affected by what had been done to her in America. She was conditioned to kill the Doctor whenever she finally met him …

A GROWN-UP MELS FINALLY MET THE DOCTOR, and took charge of the TARDIS at gunpoint. She wanted to change history by killing Adolf Hitler, but Hitler killed her first.

Mels regenerated into the River the Doctor already knew, and her conditioning kicked in. For all she was attracted to the Doctor, she kissed him with lipstick laced with poison. Yet, she also had an affinity with him and his TARDIS, and used her remaining regenerations to save him.

The Doctor left her at a hospital in the future to recover, knowing that when she was better she would come looking for him and her parents, wherever they might be in history. To do that, in 5123, River enrolled at the Luna University on a course in archaeology. But once she got her PhD, Kovarian was waiting to reinforce the conditioning and send River to kill her beloved Doctor once and for all.

The Doctor ingeniously escaped death, but to maintain the deception that she had murdered him, River willingly accepted imprisonment in the Stormcage Containment Facility – for years. The grateful Doctor secretly visited and took her out on adventures. She also escaped her cell on numerous occasions, and was even employed by her captors on missions.

When the Doctor deleted himself from every database in the universe, it appeared he had never existed, so River was pardoned and set free. With no regrets about the years she'd lost, she returned to archaeology, becoming a professor. She continued having adventures, even borrowing the TARDIS without the Doctor's knowledge.

After an extraordinary life, and extraordinary relationship with the Doctor, she set off determinedly to the assignment where a much younger Doctor met her for the first time, and she died to save him and all they were yet to share.

But the Doctor wasn't through saving her. He recorded her via a neural relay and then let her live peacefully forever after inside a computer. Even then, when the Great Intelligence threatened the Doctor's very existence, she was able to escape for one final adventure with him …

ROMANADVORATRELUNDAR, "ROMANA"

PLAYED BY **Mary Tamm, Lalla Ward**

OCCUPATION **Time Lady**

FIRST APPEARANCE *The Ribos Operation* (1978)

THERE WAS ONCE A YOUNG WOMAN with the fate of the universe in her hands.

A mysterious being called the White Guardian directed the Doctor to locate and assemble the six segments of the Key of Time before the entire universe fell into chaos. To the Doctor's dismay, he was also provided with an assistant.

The Time Lady Romanadvoratrelundar – the Doctor soon shortened her name to "Romana" – quickly and matter-of-factly got on with her job. When the Doctor doubted her credentials, she put him in his place, comparing her excellent grades at the Time Lord academy to his "scraping through".

> " *I may be inexperienced, but I did graduate from the Academy with a triple first.* "

As they set off to find the first segment on the planet Ribos, Romana diligently read up on the natives. But her naivety quickly became evident when she believed a fanciful story told by a crook because he had "such an honest face". She also hadn't anticipated how dangerous her assignment would be.

Romana learned from the Doctor as they adventured on other worlds in pursuit of the remaining segments. Once the mission was completed, Romana seemed all set to return home to Gallifrey, until the evil Black Guardian tried to take the Key to Time from them. She piloted the TARDIS to evade him as the Doctor scattered the segments once more.

Afterwards, Romana was appalled to learn the Doctor didn't know where the TARDIS was now headed. But he explained that if they didn't know where they were going, the Black Guardian wouldn't either, and so wouldn't be able to catch up with them to take his revenge. For the time being, she would have to travel on with the Doctor …

ROMANA WAS BETTER THAN THE DOCTOR AT MANY THINGS.

While regeneration for him was a traumatic and strange experience, she changed her body as easily as changing her clothes – even trying on a few options before deciding which one to stick with. She also made her own sonic screwdriver, one so superior to the Doctor's that he tried to steal it.

In her new incarnation, Romana had more child-like wonder and enthusiasm for the places they visited in time and space. Even so, she retained her withering sense of humour for those who were stupid or bullying. She also continued to learn from the Doctor, though they were becoming much more like equals. They were becoming good friends.

" Doctor, I don't want to spend the rest of my life on Gallifrey after all this ... "

She could still be naïve – helping a Jagaroth to travel back in time, without realising he intended to prevent the human race from ever existing – and she could still be scared by the strange creatures they encountered. But mostly, her adventures were fun.

Then the TARDIS was summoned back to Gallifrey. "The Time Lords want me back," Romana concluded, sadly. She didn't want to leave.

But instead of reaching Gallifrey, the TARDIS fell through a hole in space into a realm outside our own universe. There, the Doctor and Romana continued to explore. They fought marshmen and vampires, and evil humans who kept kindly creatures called Tharils as their slaves.

When the Doctor found a way back into normal space, Romana made the brave choice to stay behind without him: "I have to be my own Romana." She would create her own TARDIS and then visit the many planets in exo-space where Tharils were held prisoner. It would be her mission to free them all.

ROSE TYLER

PLAYED BY **Billie Piper**

OCCUPATION **Shop assistant, defender of the Earth**

FIRST APPEARANCE *Rose* (2005)

THERE WAS ONCE A GIRL WHO LONGED FOR SOMETHING MORE.

One day, at the dull department store where Rose worked, scary mannequins started lumbering towards her. Then a man took her hand and told her to run. Rose immediately asked questions, trying to reason things out. The strange man – the Doctor, he called himself – could see she was perceptive. He got her safely out of the building, and then blew it up.

The explosion made the news, but Rose kept quiet about what she'd seen, knowing she'd been involved in something extraordinary. Then the Doctor turned up at her flat, where they battled the disembodied arm of one the mannequins. Rose pursued the Doctor, asking more questions. Dissatisfied with what he told her, she went online to look for answers herself. She was trying to process what she'd learned when Autons attacked – and the Doctor rescued her once more.

Rose was now confronted by the fact the Doctor was an alien, whose spaceship was bigger on the inside, a man who knew impossible things about impossible creatures. Yet Rose was also intrigued by the Doctor, attracted to him, and dared to take his hand as he ran towards the secret base of the Nestene – the alien consciousness controlling the Autons.

There, Rose's courage saved the lives of her boyfriend Mickey, the Doctor, and everyone on Earth from the alien menace. Mickey was utterly terrified by what he'd experienced, but Rose was left exhilarated. Even so, when the Doctor offered her the chance to travel with him in his spaceship, she declined. After all, there was her boyfriend to look after, and her mum.

But then the Doctor told her that his ship also travelled in time. She could be back home before anyone noticed, couldn't she? Rose *raced* towards the open door …

AS THEY EXPLORED TIME AND SPACE, Rose got closer to the Doctor. He felt able to share his secret pain that he was the lone survivor of a terrible war. It made him socially awkward, but she could help with that.

When the Doctor mistakenly dropped Rose home not 12 hours but 12 months after they'd left, it clearly hurt her mum **Jackie** and boyfriend. But Rose never reconsidered travelling with the Doctor. He needed her. Often her compassion and the easy friendships she struck up helped solve the problems they faced – notably when, through Rose's influence, a Dalek developed emotions!

When the Doctor sent Rose home in the TARDIS to protect her from an invasion of Daleks in the year 200,100, she was determined to help him anyway. Managing to gain access to the TARDIS's incredible powers, she returned to the future transformed into the Bad Wolf, a being that effortlessly destroyed a fleet of Dalek saucers and brought a friend back from the dead. But such extraordinary power was burning her up. The Doctor took it from her with a kiss, saving her life at the cost of his own.

"I think I know a thing or two about aliens."

The newly regenerated Doctor soon won Rose over and they enjoyed more adventures. But, while stopping Daleks and Cybermen from ransacking London, she became trapped with her family and boyfriend on a parallel Earth, with no chance of getting back to the Doctor.

She got on with defending this parallel world, taking over its version of Torchwood. Spotting a looming crisis, she worked out how to teleport back to her own Earth to help the Doctor and his other friends defeat a plot by Davros, creator of the Daleks. Rose was a soldier now, yet the Doctor still depended on her compassion.

During this adventure, a second, fully human Doctor was created, who needed Rose's guidance – or so the original Doctor said. Rose had to be the one to decide, and she did. She would spend her life with the human Doctor on the parallel world, and never see the Time Lord she'd loved again.

ROSITA

PLAYED BY **Velile Tshabalala**

OCCUPATION **Victorian Londoner**

FIRST APPEARANCE *The Next Doctor* (2008)

ONCE UPON A TIME IN LONDON, a woman was attacked by a metal monster – a Cyberman. She thought she was going to die but then a man came to her rescue, a man who said his name was the Doctor.

Grateful to her saviour, Rosita became his companion. She helped him hunt the Cybermen through London, and she soothed the Doctor when he had terrible dreams, waking at night in a state of terror.

Rosita was bold and brave and practical. When another man claiming to be the Doctor turned up, her response was matter of fact: "Well, there can't be two of you."

She was always telling off her Doctor and chivvying him along, encouraging him. When he suggested that it was not suitable for her, as a woman, to help him break into a house as part of their investigation, she gave him short shrift. In fact, she couldn't bear to be left behind – she'd go frantic with worry for him. Then she thought her Doctor had been killed by the Cybermen. When it turned out that he'd survived, she surprised him with a big hug.

She was a woman of passion, and even knocked the wicked **Mercy Hartigan** to the ground with a single punch. But Rosita also had a strong sense of right and wrong. Despite the investigation, she was wary of snooping through someone else's possessions.

She was also good at making sense of the mystery from the clues they uncovered. She was the one to suggest that the late Reverend Fairchild had been murdered by the Cybermen, and that her Doctor was really a human man called Jackson Lake.

Her local knowledge guided the real Doctor to Ingleby Workhouse, which the Cybermen had taken over, and then helped him rescue the children held prisoner there. After that, she bravely went back into the workhouse to find Jackson and help him escape. She would always remain his faithful companion, whoever he really was.

SALLY SPARROW

PLAYED BY **Carey Mulligan**

OCCUPATION **Investigator, book and DVD seller**

FIRST APPEARANCE *Blink* (2007)

THERE WAS ONCE A YOUNG WOMAN WHO LOVED OLD THINGS.

One night, she climbed the high fence round a spooky old house, to take photographs. Hidden under the wallpaper, she found a message written to her – by name.

Freaked out, Sally went back with her friend Kathy Nightingale. But Kathy disappeared, apparently sent back in time by statues and living the rest of her life in the past.

Even more freaked out, Sally tried to share what she'd witnessed with Kathy's brother, Larry. He was engrossed in his pet project to join a series of DVD "Easter eggs" of a strange man addressing the camera, into a single clip.

Sally went to the police about her missing friend. A young detective inspector chatted her up. When she saw him later that day, he was an old man. He too had been sent back into the past, where he had been instructed to publish the DVD "Easter eggs". Sally realised that the 17 DVDs on which they appeared were all the DVDs she owned. The clips were *another* message aimed at her.

She met Larry at the old house, where they played the footage – and Sally had a conversation with it. The man on screen, the Doctor, was reading from the transcript that Sally could see Larry writing as she spoke. He was a time traveller who needed to recover his TARDIS from the Weeping Angels, deadly aliens who could only move when unobserved.

As the Weeping Angels attacked, Sally tried to stare them out, and she and Larry went down to the basement to send the TARDIS to the Doctor. As the blue box disappeared, the Angels surrounding it saw each other and became harmless stone.

A year later, the obsessed Sally had diligently gathered all evidence of what she'd been through. Then she spotted the Doctor; for him, the adventure hadn't happened yet. Sally handed over her evidence, which would enable him, when the time came, to put into action all the strange things that had happened to her. "Goodbye, Doctor," she said, and took Larry's hand, ready to begin a new life.

SAMANTHA BRIGGS

PLAYED BY **Pauline Collins**

OCCUPATION **Forthright sister**

FIRST APPEARANCE *The Faceless Ones* (1967)

THERE WAS ONCE A YOUNG WOMAN who would not take no for an answer.

When her brother disappeared while on holiday in Rome, Samantha decided to track him down. The police confirmed he'd not stayed at *any* hotel in the city, and yet Samantha had received a postcard from him, posted there.

The police lacked the resources to investigate further so Samantha left Liverpool for Gatwick Airport, where she confronted the staff of Chameleon Tours, who had organised her brother's holiday. They weren't very forthcoming. But, as she waited by the kiosk, a flight to Zurich was called and Samantha spotted something odd. Passengers were encouraged to write postcards home *before* they boarded the flight, which the tour company would then post for them. If her brother had done the same, perhaps he'd never got as far as Rome!

With no one else willing to help her, Samantha teamed up with "a right weirdie" called the Doctor and his handsome young friend Jamie, who were also investigating Chameleon Tours for their own missing friends. Samantha boldly went off to search the company's hanger herself, compelling Jamie to join her. Together they found 50 postcards written by passengers in advance of their flights, all ready to be posted. It was hard evidence of foul play, which upset Samantha, though she was too proud to admit she was crying.

Soon it emerged that people were being abducted and duplicated by aliens. Despite the clear danger, Samantha bought a ticket to Rome, prepared to risk an unknown fate to find out what had happened to her brother. At the last minute, Jamie stole her ticket and took her place.

Samantha still wouldn't sit idly by. She now worked with the airport authorities to track down a group of human hostages the aliens had hidden. By discovering them in time, Samantha and her friends forced the aliens to back down and make peace.

Job done, Samantha kissed Jamie goodbye and then waited for her brother to arrive back at the airport, one of the 50,000 abducted people she had helped to free.

SARA KINGDOM

PLAYED BY **Jean Marsh, May Warden**

OCCUPATION **Space Security Service agent**

FIRST APPEARANCE *The Daleks' Master Plan* (1965–66)

ONCE UPON A TIME IN THE FUTURE, there was a woman who knew her duty.

As a special agent of Earth's Space Security Service, Sara was tasked with tracking down three traitors and recovering a rare mineral element they had stolen. She soon found one of the traitors and shot him down. She knew her duty, no matter that he was her brother!

She soon tracked down the other traitors – the Doctor and Steven Taylor – but all three were accidentally transmitted far across space to the planet Mira. The cynical, sensible Sara could hardly believe it. Nor did she want to believe the Doctor and Steven's story, that Mavic Chen, the Guardian of the Solar System, was the real traitor. Chen had secretly allied himself with the Daleks, and needed the rare mineral to power a terrible Dalek weapon: the Time Destructor.

When the Daleks arrived on Mira, Sara was forced to believe the Doctor's story and determined to stop Chen's evil scheme, whatever that might take. She was an efficient, well-trained fighter, and wary of trusting anyone. She could quickly be exasperated by the Doctor's eccentricities, but also came to enjoy her time with him as they worked to save Earth and its empire.

Eventually, the Doctor got her to Kembel for a final showdown with the Daleks. Sara approached the problem with cool detachment, asking Steven to explain how to work his power impulse compass so she could take over its operation if he was killed. But her travels had changed her; she dared to trust the imprisoned alien delegates, releasing them so that they would escape back to their own people and raise forces against the Daleks. She also refused to follow the Doctor's orders to return to the TARDIS where she would be safe. She helped him as he grappled with the activated Time Destructor.

Tragically, the terrible weapon aged Sara to death. But it also destroyed the Daleks. She had, for one final incredible time, done her duty.

SARAH JANE SMITH

PLAYED BY **Elisabeth Sladen**

OCCUPATION **Journalist**

FIRST APPEARANCE *The Time Warrior* (1973–74)

THERE WAS ONCE A GIRL WHO LOST EVERYTHING.

When she was just three months old, Sarah's parents died in a car accident. Sarah wouldn't discover until much later that they had sacrificed their lives to thwart a wicked creature called the Trickster, who had designs on the world. The orphan girl was brought up by her aunt, Lavinia, a well-respected, hard-working virologist.

When Sarah was 13, she suffered another terrible loss, witnessing the death of her best friend in an accident. It changed Sarah forever, making her realise how precious life was and that she should fight to make it better. This helped to shape her career path: Sarah became an investigative journalist. She was smart and diligent, and also a vehement feminist.

" There's nothing 'only' about being a girl. "

While her aunt was away on a lecture tour, Sarah used her name to sneak into a top secret government establishment employing leading scientists, some of whom had recently disappeared. Bravely, she pursued the story, following a suspicious man called the Doctor into his old police box.

Sarah found herself back in the 13th century, and after gathering her wits helped the Doctor defeat a wicked Sontaran called Lynx. The Doctor returned Sarah to her own time, where they discovered London was at the mercy of dinosaurs. Her adventurous instincts, commitment to help others and fierce resolve to find the truth meant that the life of a space-time traveller suited her as much as it did the Doctor.

Intelligent, brave and always asking the right questions, Sarah was a great help to the Doctor. She was eager to improve the lot of the women she met on her adventures, introducing the idea of women's liberation to the enslaved kitchen staff of a 13th-century castle and to Queen Thalira of the planet Peladon.

SARAH CONTINUED TO TRAVEL WITH THE DOCTOR after he regenerated, facing many perils. She was there at the creation of the Daleks and helped the Doctor battle an Osirian god, where her detailed knowledge of ancient Egyptian lore and her skill with a rifle both came in handy.

In her time with the Doctor, Sarah was possessed by villains, temporarily blinded, dropped from great heights and tortured for a Sontaran scientific experiment, but she rarely complained, often responding with wit and kindness.

After she left the TARDIS, Sarah continued to investigate strange phenomena and bravely expose the truth. A little while after she'd left him, the Doctor sent her a present – a robot dog called K9, who assisted her on her adventures. She carried on with her life, though no one could ever quite match up to the man she'd travelled with in space and time.

> " **Pain and loss, they define us as much as happiness or love. Whether it's a world, or a relationship, everything has its time. And everything ends.** "

Then, when she investigated a strange school, there he was again – looking younger than ever. Sarah was deeply hurt that he hadn't mentioned her name to his latest companions, and was initially jealous and difficult with **Rose Tyler**. But she was too compassionate for any ill-feeling to last. Sarah was soon helping the Doctor and Rose defeat alien invaders, and she promised Rose a sympathetic ear when the time came for *her* to leave the Doctor.

Her reunion with the Doctor allowed Sarah to confront and deal with the losses she'd suffered in life, so she could connect again with other people. She adopted an alien-manufactured boy, Luke, and he and his school friends became dependable allies in her adventures. She became a mentor to young Rani Chandra, who aspired to be an investigative journalist just like Sarah. Later, Sarah adopted another alien child, a girl called Sky.

With this family around her, and armed with a sonic lipstick, Sarah continued to investigate mysteries, expose secrets and defend the world in style.

"SUSAN FOREMAN"

PLAYED BY **Carole Ann Ford**

OCCUPATION **The Doctor's granddaughter**

FIRST APPEARANCE *An Unearthly Child* (1963)

ONCE UPON A TIME, a girl and her grandfather travelled in time and space. They visited the Rings of Akhaten, and the planet Quinnis in the Fourth Universe (where they almost lost their ship), and got into a fight with Henry VIII, the king of a small province on the planet Earth.

Their wanderings weren't always fun. Sometimes there were misunderstandings between the girl and her grandfather, because of the gulf in their ages. And while her grandfather was always keen to keep moving on so that no one could ever find them, the girl longed for a place to call home.

Earth was primitive compared to some worlds they'd known, but the people there bore a physical resemblance to their own. The girl felt a connection to the place so, against her grandfather's better judgement, they spent five months in London in the year 1963. The girl took a name for herself in her new life: Susan.

Trying to seem "normal", Susan attended the Coal Hill secondary school a short walk from their ship. She claimed that her surname was Foreman, after the proprietor of the junkyard in which the ship was hidden, and that her grandfather was a Doctor. She came to think of her stay on 20th-century Earth as one of the happiest of her life but, being alien, she couldn't hope to blend in entirely. Often she would bamboozle her tutors with both the range of her knowledge and the inexplicable gaps within it. Two of her teachers were concerned for their mysterious pupil – and intensely curious about her – and so they followed her home.

The two teachers stumbled into the ship, which Susan had named TARDIS, and the girl's grandfather took them all away from the 20th century. For Susan and the Doctor – and the entire multiverse, for that matter – things would never be the same …

THE FOUR OF THEM SURVIVED MANY EPIC VOYAGES together through time and space and the unknown. They became good friends. Susan's naivety sometimes landed her travelling companions in trouble, but her alien knowledge and powers as often helped them out of a crisis.

Trapped and helpless on the world of the Daleks, Susan was the least affected by radiation in the air. While her grandfather and the teachers sickened, she bravely set out into an eerie, petrified jungle to get the drugs that would save all their lives. Another time, on another world, her telepathic abilities helped resolve a conflict between humans and Sensorites.

But Susan still yearned for a place to call home, and knew her grandfather would never settle anywhere. Then, on the same small island on Earth, she fell in love with a young man. She knew she could only explore her feelings by staying with him on Earth, in one place. But could she really put her own needs and happiness above caring for her grandfather in their wanderers' life?

" You see, David, Grandfather's old now. He needs me. "

Before she could truly decide for herself, her grandfather chose Susan's welfare above his own. He left that time and place in their ramshackle ship, leaving her with David to be happy – and to be home. But a part of Susan stayed with the Doctor, influencing his choice of those who joined him in the TARDIS ever after.

Many years later, Susan – now a woman – saw her grandfather once more, when they were both brought back to their own planet by her grandfather's old and wicked teacher.

She still had her telepathic powers, sensing her grandfather's presence before she found him. But what took her by surprise was how much he had changed. For as well as the crotchety old man she knew so well, she also met three of the men he would become – including one who seemed younger than she was!

TASHA LEM

PLAYED BY **Orla Brady**

OCCUPATION **Mother Superious**

FIRST APPEARANCE *The Time of the Doctor* (2013)

THERE WAS ONCE A WOMAN DESPERATE TO STOP A WAR.

As head of the powerful Church of the Papal Mainframe, Tasha was first to respond to the mysterious message broadcast from the planet Trenzalore, which made all sentient beings afraid. While other species such as the Daleks and Cybermen sought to attack the source of the message, Tasha's spaceship – a huge flying church – established forcefields that would protect the level 2 human colony on the planet's surface. Her shields maintained an uneasy truce, blocking the other species and avoiding bloodshed.

Then the Doctor asked her if he could investigate. He and Tasha had history; he knew she'd spent her whole life fighting a psychopathic part of her personality. Tasha agreed, but with conditions: he was to go for an hour, and not cause any trouble. She was then furious when he translated the message for all to hear. It was from his own, long-lost people, and if he replied, the Time Lords would re-emerge into this universe and the horrific Time War would start anew.

Tasha quickly dedicated all her resources to ensuring that the Doctor would never answer the message. "Silence will fall," she declared. She and the Doctor both defended the human colony from attack by the other species. Over the next 300 years, they met up regularly to discuss progress. Tasha also supplied the Doctor with sweets. Then the Daleks attacked the Papal Mainframe and slaughtered her people. Tasha died in agony, calling out the Doctor's name. The Daleks took control of her dead body, using her in a trap for the Doctor.

But Tasha's will was strong enough to resist the Dalek conditioning. Unchanging, she continued to fight alongside the Doctor to maintain the peace.

By then, after 1,000 years, the Doctor was dying. Tasha took command of his TARDIS and travelled to Earth to fetch the Doctor's friend, **Clara Oswald**. It was Clara who broke the stalemate, and the conflict was finally ended – but without Tasha's compassion, she would never have been given the chance.

TEGAN JOVANKA

PLAYED BY **Janet Fielding**

OCCUPATION **Air stewardess**

FIRST APPEARANCE *Logopolis* (1981)

THERE WAS ONCE A YOUNG WOMAN WHO YEARNED TO FLY.

Tegan grew up on a farm in Australia, and although it was hardly the outback, her family owned a plane. She developed a love for flying and aircraft, and grew up fiercely independent – if not always very organised. When her aunt's car had a flat tyre, the self-sufficient Tegan was determined to fix it herself rather than finding a mechanic to do it for her.

Tegan's determination was also the result of her new job as an air stewardess, which required her to solve problems practically. She had learned all the aircraft procedures and instructions by heart, and tried to respond to crises with a cool, professional air.

That wasn't always easy. Finally admitting they needed help with the car if she was to make her flight in time, Tegan tried a nearby police telephone box – and then got lost inside what turned out to be an enormous time machine. She was soon transported to another planet. Meanwhile, Tegan's beloved aunt was murdered by the evil Master, who then threatened the safety of the whole universe. Tegan helped the Doctor to stop him.

The Doctor died while preventing the Master's wicked scheme, and then regenerated into a younger, more agreeable man. Tegan gave him short shrift when he failed to get her back to Heathrow Airport and her longed-for job, but proved a loyal and resourceful member of his crew.

Terrible things happened – Tegan was possessed by a hateful alien creature called the Mara, and her friend Adric was killed while battling Cybermen – but there were good times too. She danced the Charleston in 1925, and formed a strong bond with her fellow companion, **Nyssa**. Tegan, the keen flyer, even successfully piloted the TARDIS, if more by luck than judgment.

So when the Doctor finally got her back to Heathrow Airport, she had mixed feelings – and was surprised and sad to be left behind when the TARDIS departed.

TEGAN'S JOB AS AN AIR STEWARDESS DIDN'T LAST LONG. She was fired for reasons she never owned up to, but was reunited with the Doctor by chance after a trip to Amsterdam that turned into another horrifying adventure.

She rejoined the TARDIS and resumed her travels through time and space – and into danger. Tegan was again possessed by the evil Mara. Soon after, the Doctor took on a new companion, Turlough, who Tegan took against. And she was hurt and saddened by her friend Nyssa's choice to leave them for an arduous life on a hospital in space.

But there were brighter moments. Tegan enjoyed dressing up for a party on board a spacecraft thrown by the alien Eternals, and enjoyed meeting many of the Doctor's former companions when they were all brought to the Doctor's home planet – though she was quick to protest when the First Doctor suggested she make herself useful and get everyone drinks. Tegan was also delighted to catch up with her grandfather on another of her adventures.

" I'm not in the mood for playing silly games. "

But the dangers and death she faced were taking their toll, and Tegan was always brutally honest. After a particularly bloody battle with the Daleks in the London of her own time, she decided to leave the TARDIS. "My Aunt Vanessa said, when I became an air stewardess, 'If you stop enjoying it, give it up,'" she told the Doctor. "It's stopped being fun."

He was sad to lose her, and determined to act on what she'd said to mend his ways. But soon after the TARDIS had dematerialised, Tegan came running back – just too late to change her mind. Shocked to have lost him for good, she quoted his own words back to herself as encouragement for her new life on Earth: "Brave heart, Tegan."

TRINITY WELLS

PLAYED BY **Lachele Carl**

OCCUPATION **Newsreader**

FIRST APPEARANCE *Aliens of London* (2005)

THERE WAS ONCE A WOMAN WHOSE JOB WAS TO BE CALM IN A CRISIS.

Trinity Wells was a newsreader for American network AMNN, lending gravitas and authority to events she covered.

That skill and experience came to the fore when an alien spaceship collided with the iconic clocktower of the Palace of Westminster in London, England, and then crashed into the river Thames. Soon, contact with aliens had led to panic and looting, and a national emergency was declared. Trinity was just as shaken by the events as everyone else, but she got on with her job, reporting calmly and succinctly the known facts. Even when the United Nations gave the nuclear codes to the British Government to help fight back against the aliens, Trinity kept her cool. She was a reassuring presence in moments of chaos and mayhem.

That's probably why her network had her report on strange events ever after. That Christmas, Trinity was again on air as a gigantic Sycorax spaceship parked over London. She was in the studio when Prime Minister Harold Saxon announced he had made contact with an alien race, and she informed the public that people were abandoning their cars equipped with ATMOS satellite navigation, because of a release of deadly gases.

For all the strange things she reported on, things could get pretty strange in the studio, too. Trinity was reporting on the US President announcing his plan to end the recession when she and every other human being were transformed temporarily into the Master. For Trinity, it was all in a day's work. No doubt she was still reporting when a vast red planet appeared in the skies over Earth soon after.

VICKI

PLAYED BY **Maureen O'Brien**

OCCUPATION **Orphan**

FIRST APPEARANCE *The Rescue* (1965)

THERE WAS ONCE A GIRL WHO LOST EVERYTHING.

Vicki had a fun childhood on Earth in the late 25th century, with just an hour a week's education by machine. Aged 10, she took a certificate of education in medicine, physics and chemistry. She also knew some history.

But life soon changed drastically. Her mother died and her father accepted a job on the planet Astra. As he and Vicki journeyed there, their spaceship crashed on the barren planet Dido. Her father and the rest of the crew were killed soon after at a meeting with Dido's inhabitants. Vicki had been ill and so missed the meeting. The only other survivor was a gruff man called Bennett.

"Supposing you do what I say for once?"

When the visiting Doctor revealed that Bennett had murdered Vicki's father and everyone else to cover up an earlier crime, Vicki gratefully joined the TARDIS crew.

Vicki had a strong sense of justice. She instinctively swapped goblets of poison prepared by **Locusta** to save an innocent Roman slave, and complained when the Doctor made her dress like a boy to keep her safe in the 12th century Holy Land, where girls still risked enslavement. On the planet Xeros, Vicki helped organise a revolution, and when the TARDIS accidentally left her behind in a strange house on Earth, she bravely stowed away on a Dalek time machine until she caught up with her friends.

When the TARDIS landed near Troy at the end of the famous siege, Vicki was excited to meet the heroes she'd learned about as a child. But she also knew the awful fate awaiting the city. When her warnings were ignored, she was at least able to save a young Trojan called Troilus, and decided to stay with him on Earth. In doing so, she became part of the legends she had enjoyed as a child.

QUEEN VICTORIA

PLAYED BY **Pauline Collins**

OCCUPATION **Queen**

FIRST APPEARANCE *Tooth and Claw* (2006)

ONCE UPON A TIME IN SCOTLAND, a trap was laid for a queen.

On her way to Balmoral Castle, Victoria was forced to stop overnight at the Torchwood Estate, a house Victoria had never been to before, but which had been a favourite of her late husband's.

A group of evil monks had secretly taken over the house. They served an alien werewolf who planned to bite Victoria, infecting her bloodline. However, a strange man called the Doctor convinced the Queen that he'd been sent to protect her. His companion, **Rose Tyler**, wore strange clothes that shocked the sensibilities of Victoria's soldiers, but the sensible, serious Queen took them in her stride.

One monk cornered Victoria, but after six attempts on her life already, she now carried a pistol. The monk didn't think a mere woman would dare shoot. Victoria stared him down fearlessly. "The correct form of address is 'Your Majesty'," she said before she pulled the trigger. It was hardly good form for the queen to shoot a would-be assassin, so she announced that one of her soldiers had done so.

Victoria wouldn't believe in the werewolf until she saw it with her own eyes. She also didn't like the way the Doctor and Rose delighted in this adventure; she wanted nothing to do with such strange and terrible things.

But the Doctor then revealed that there was a trap within the trap. Victoria's late husband had believed the werewolf legends and prepared a response. The huge Koh-i-Noor diamond he had given her as a present could be fitted to complete a special weapon which finally destroyed the menace.

Later, Victoria acknowledged that the Doctor and Rose had saved her life – and the British Empire – and dubbed them Sir Doctor of TARDIS and Lady Rose of the Powell Estate. But horrified by their gleeful attitude to alien menace, she then banished them from her kingdom and established the Torchwood organisation to defend Earth from extra-terrestrial threats – which, to her mind, included the Doctor.

VICTORIA WATERFIELD

PLAYED BY **Deborah Watling**

OCCUPATION **Orphan**

FIRST APPEARANCE *The Evil of the Daleks* (1967)

ONCE UPON A TIME IN AN OLD HOUSE, a girl was held prisoner by monsters.

Victoria had grown up happily in the mid 19th century until her mother died. She and her father were taken in by Professor Theodore Maxtible, moving into his fine house just outside Canterbury. There Victoria made good friends with Maxtible's daughter Ruth and the servant girl Mollie. Another servant, Kemal, was devoted to her too.

But Maxtible had secretly embroiled Victoria's father in a scientific endeavour that led to death and disaster. Alien Daleks invaded the house and took Victoria hostage to force the two men to work for them. She was taken to their planet, Skaro, where the Doctor and his friend Jamie rescued her, but both Kemal and her beloved father were killed. The Doctor promised the dying Waterfield that he would look after Victoria, and so invited her aboard the TARDIS.

It was a strange and often scary experience for the young orphan. There were more monsters – Cybermen, Yeti, Ice Warriors and killer seaweed. And then there were the clothes! Victoria adopted shorter skirts because they were more practical for her adventures than a 19th-century frock, but she still felt uneasy in something so revealing and was shocked by the tight-fitting clothes worn by women in the Britain of the far future.

For all she was fearful, Victoria would always try her best to help. She would argue her case with anyone, took risks to help the Doctor, and even declined the safety of a Tibetan monastery to share the dangers faced by her friends.

But the constant terror ate away at her, and she longed to find somewhere peaceful to call home. On 20th-century Earth, long after her own time, she found just such a place with Maggie and Frank Harris – the latter a kindly scientist, a bit like her father.

She was torn about leaving the Doctor and Jamie, but once her decision was made she stood by it, and said a firm but fond farewell.

BRIGADIER WINIFRED BAMBERA

PLAYED BY **Angela Bruce**

OCCUPATION **UNIT brigadier**

FIRST APPEARANCE *Battlefield* (1989)

THERE WAS ONCE A WOMAN WITH A JOB TO DO.

Brigadier Winifred Bambera was gruff with those around her. She did not like being lied to or kept out of the loop. So she wasn't overjoyed to meet a scientific advisor to UNIT she hadn't been briefed about: the Doctor. And, when escorting a nuclear missile through countryside, she did not appreciate being attacked by knights from another dimension …

Winifred was courageous under fire, reassuring members of the public that she was in charge and everything was OK. When one posh knight refused to answer her questions – considering her a peasant – she literally fought to change his mind. Winifred won their battle and the knight's respect.

> **You call me 'My lady' once more and I'll break your nose.**

Soon, the knight had fallen for this formidable woman, and she warmed to him too. Together, they fought an invading army, him following her orders. That included when she told him to take the wheel of the car they were in, so she could stand up through the sunroof and shoot at the attacking army with a sub-machine gun! Even her enemies declared her "magnificent".

Winifred didn't share the knights' zeal for battle. She regretted the loss of life, even of her enemies. But, thanks to the Doctor, their foes surrendered. The Doctor trusted Winifred to take charge of the evil witch, Morgaine, and her troublesome son, Mordred.

The battle over, Winifred relaxed enough to join Ace and other women on a fun daytrip in the Doctor's car – leaving him and the other men to do the housework and have dinner ready for their return. Characteristically, she remained in her uniform, and reminded **Ace** not to break any traffic laws.

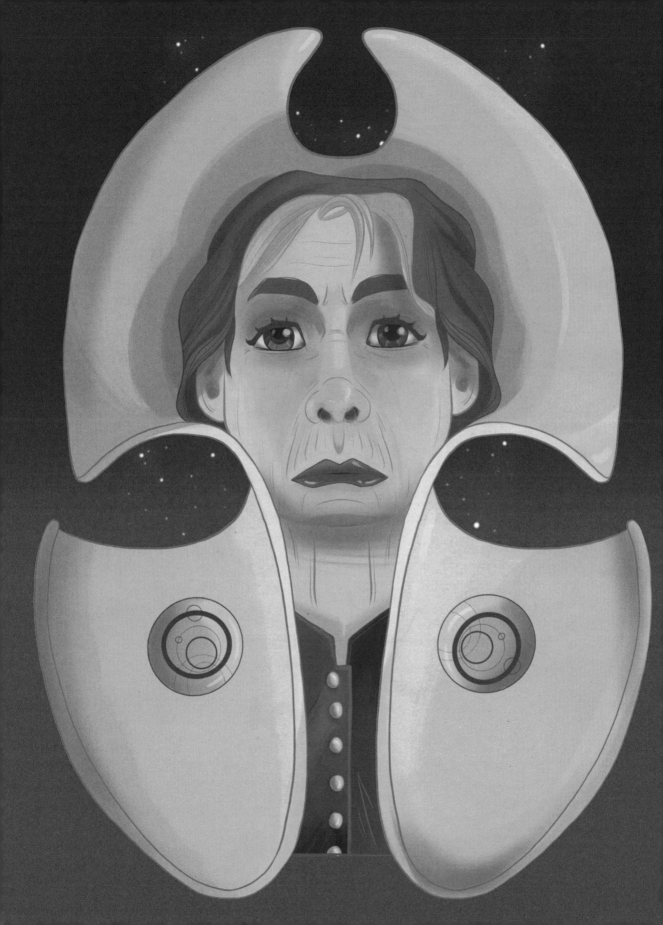

"THE WOMAN"

PLAYED BY **Claire Bloom**

OCCUPATION **Mysterious Time Lady**

FIRST APPEARANCE *The End of Time* (2009)

IN WHAT WERE NEARLY THE LAST DAYS OF PLANET EARTH, a mysterious woman appeared to the Doctor's old friend Wilf Mott.

Wilf first met her in a church where the stained-glass window included a picture of the TARDIS. The mysterious woman, smartly dressed in white, told him this related to events in the 1300s, but she also knew the future. "Perhaps he's coming back," she said … and disappeared.

Wilf saw her again on his TV at home, though only he could see her. She knew Wilf had been a soldier, and had never killed a man. She told him he would have to take up arms and that he might yet save the Doctor's life, so long as Wilf kept his conversation with the woman secret.

So Wilf pocketed his gun and tracked the Doctor down. The woman appeared to Wilf again but would not tell him who she was, only that she'd been lost.

In fact, she was one of two Time Lords to vote against the "Ultimate Sanction" – a plan to destroy the vortex of time and everyone in the universe on the last day of the Time War. She and her compatriot were punished for this opposition, made to follow Rassilon, Lord President of the Time Lords, with their heads in their hands.

When the Doctor, armed with Wilf's gun, faced Rassilon, he saw the woman standing there and the sight profoundly affected him. He turned the gun away from his enemies and instead shot the Immortality Gate, sending Rassilon and other Time Lords – including the woman – back into the Time War.

The tragedy did not end there, for in directing Wilf to join the Doctor, the woman helped bring about the Doctor's death. To save Wilf, he accepted a fatal dose of radiation.

The woman knew the Doctor well, and wielded awesome power, but who was she? Perhaps the Doctor's mother, or his beloved granddaughter **Susan Foreman** in a new incarnation?

Only the Doctor can say.

YASMIN "YAZ" KHAN

PLAYED BY **Mandip Gill**

OCCUPATION **Probationary police officer**

FIRST APPEARANCE *Series 11, Episode 1* (2018)

ONCE UPON A TIME, a girl was just beginning the most extraordinary adventure ...

Yaz was training to be a police officer in her hometown of Sheffield when her whole life suddenly and radically changed. She loved her job because it meant she got to help people and because it took her out of her comfort zone. With an eye for detail and a quick, logical mind, she was looking for bigger challenges – which is exactly what she got when she met the Doctor!

Soon she was helping solve mysteries, fight monsters and help people all across time and space. In many ways, she and the Doctor were kindred spirits, bravely stepping forward to assist those in need, and to confront those threatening harm.

Her police training made her physically tough, but Yaz was also fearless. She refused to be bullied or intimidated by anyone, and liked to think she would be the first to step into any dangerous situation to try and calm things down. Yaz had a taste for thrilling adventure, but was skilled in resolving disputes amicably.

Joining the TARDIS presented Yaz with all the challenge – and wonders – she could ask for.

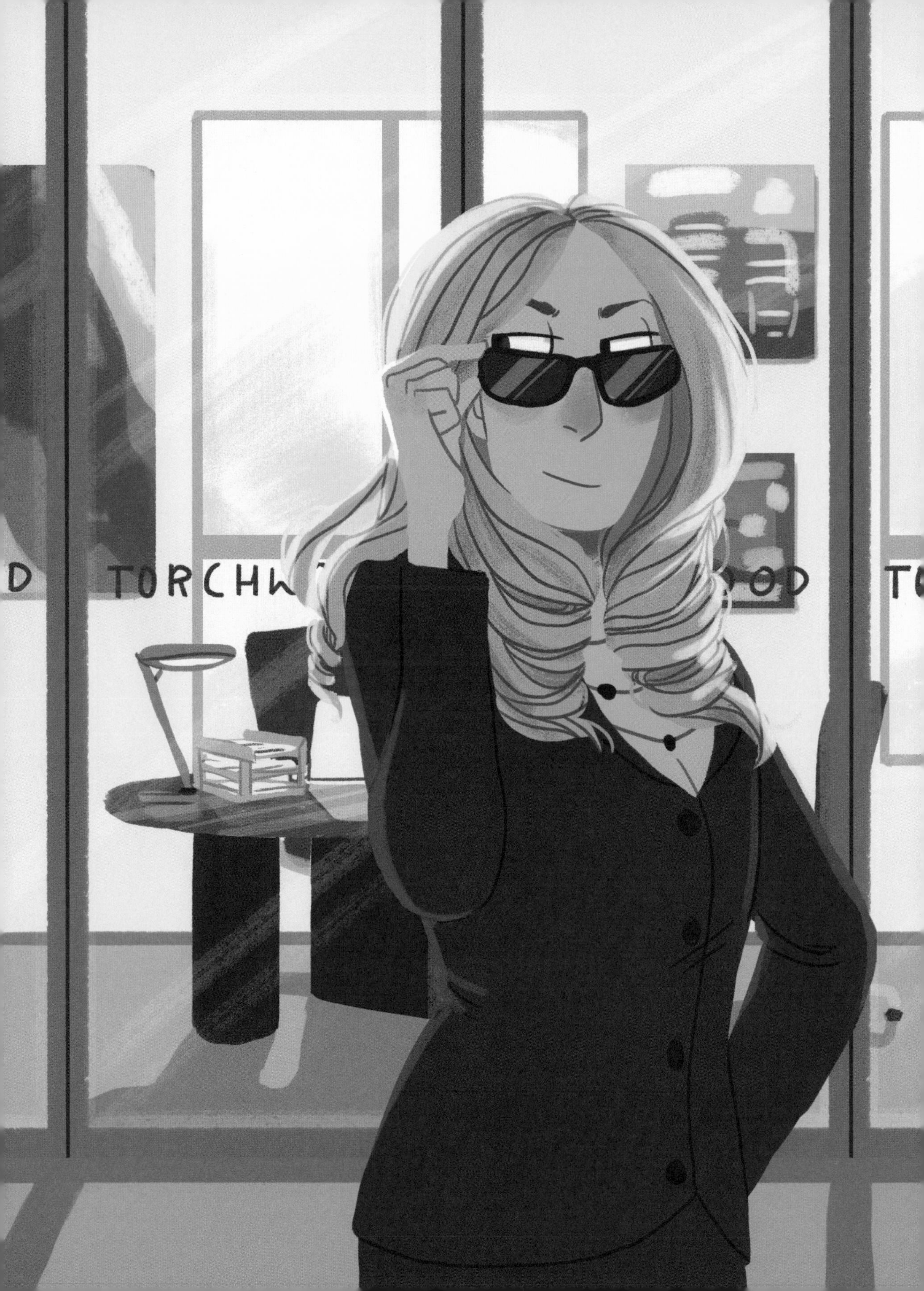

YVONNE HARTMAN

PLAYED BY **Tracy-Ann Oberman**

OCCUPATION **Torchwood One Project Leader**

FIRST APPEARANCE *Army of Ghosts* (2006)

THERE WAS ONCE A WOMAN WHO KNEW HER DUTY, even when everything else had been stripped away.

Yvonne led Torchwood's investigation into a radar black spot, a zone of weird properties over London's docks. Torchwood had already built a skyscraper up to and around the black spot – the iconic building of One Canada Square, Canary Wharf. Then, from the weird zone there emerged a large sphere, one with its own strange properties. People in its vicinity wanted to run away.

Yvonne was in charge of studying the sphere, and of reopening the zone through which it had come, which had potential as a major new power source. In opening this breach in reality, Yvonne's team drew forth hundreds of thousands of "ghosts", who appeared all round the world. Yet she was resolute that this would be a patriotic endeavour: she hoped to re-establish the British Empire.

She was a good leader, knowing her staff by their first names. But Yvonne had not asked questions about building work going on near her office, and failed to notice when members of her staff started acting oddly. They'd been taken over by the "ghosts" – in fact an invasion force of Cybermen – who now took over her project. For all Yvonne had worked with strange alien technology, she was squeamish when presented with the truth of what the Cybermen had done to her staff: plugging technology directly into their brains.

Soon, she was taken away to be upgraded. Unlike **Jackie Tyler**, Yvonne quickly understood the full horror of what this involved. She went to her upgrade repeating the belief she'd lived by: that she had done her duty. Whatever else was taken from her, that mantra remained. In the shell of a Cyberman, she fought the other Cybermen, defending the breach in reality on behalf of Queen and country, while an oily, blue tear ran down her metal face.

ZOE HERIOT

PLAYED BY **Wendy Padbury**

OCCUPATION **Parapsychology librarian, astrophysicist, astrometricist**

FIRST APPEARANCE *The Wheel in Space* (1968)

ONCE UPON A TIME, a clever girl was eager to learn new things.

At a young age, Zoe qualified with honours in astrophysics and mathematics, and was a first-class astrometricist. This led to a job in the parapsychology library of Space Station W3. As well as being a genius, she had an eidetic memory and was rarely wrong in her calculations.

Zoe was less competent on pre-century history, and her dependence on logic and plain statement of facts could make her seem cold. One colleague referred to her as "All brain and no heart." The fact that this hurt Zoe showed it wasn't true.

When she met the Doctor and his friend Jamie, she saw an opportunity to learn from them both. If she sometimes patronised Jamie for being from the 18th century and lacking knowledge of science and technology, she savoured his insights into history and his impish sense of fun.

Zoe could be rebellious, too, and when told she couldn't join the Doctor and Jamie in the TARDIS, she stowed away. She was soon helping to defeat monsters, outwitting the intelligence tests of the alien Krotons and calculating how to destroy an invasion fleet of Cybermen in a chain reaction of explosions. Zoe was also adept at physical combat: when a fictional superhero, the Karkus, came to life and attacked her, she deftly threw him over her shoulder and forced him to submit.

Finally there was a challenge that she and the Doctor couldn't solve themselves. To stop the evil War Lord, the Doctor had no choice but to call in the help of his own people, the Time Lords – knowing they would punish him for stealing the TARDIS and interfering in the affairs of others. Zoe tried to help the Doctor escape, but in vain. The Time Lords sent her back to the Space Station, erasing all her memories of travelling in the TARDIS.

She was left with a lingering sense that she'd forgotten something important … but soon dismissed the thought and went back to her work.

THE DOCTOR

PLAYED BY **Jodie Whittaker and others**

OCCUPATION **Time Lord**

FIRST APPEARANCE *An Unearthly Child* (1963)

ONCE, A VERY LONG TIME AGO, my granddaughter and I stole a TARDIS and fled into time and space.

I loved exploring new worlds, even when it was dangerous. In fact, I once pretended that the TARDIS was broken, just so we could have a look round an alien city, supposedly for the chemical element needed to repair it! That was how I first met the malevolent Daleks.

However, my granddaughter, **Susan Foreman**, wanted to settle on Earth – and did so. Despite the loss I felt, I kept on travelling, finding new friends to join me.

Those friends questioned my motives, arguing that it wasn't enough just to observe the people living on the planets we visited. We should also try to help these people, and battle the monsters and evil that threatened them.

I was hesitant at first, insisting we couldn't get involved. But whenever I met the Daleks, I was ready to battle them. Soon, I was seeking out confrontations with those who would oppress, attack and invade.

As a result, my own people – the Time Lords – caught up with me and put me on trial. They considered getting involved in the affairs of others a serious crime. But I argued passionately that I had a duty to battle evil wherever I might find it.

To my surprise, although I was punished, my people heeded my argument. I was forced to regenerate and exiled to Earth in the 20th century, at a time when that planet faced many perils and needed me to defend it. My people also sent me on missions to other worlds.

When I saved my own planet – and the universe – from destruction at the hands of a deranged Time Lord named Omega, my punishment was ended and I was again allowed the use of my TARDIS.

ONE DAY, I FOUND MYSELF BACK ON SKARO, planet of the Daleks. The Time Lords had another task for me, this time to stop the Daleks ever being created. Unwilling to commit such an act of genocide, I opted instead to delay the Daleks' development by a few thousand years … an act that would come back to haunt not only me but the entire universe.

I continued my adventures, helping people and thwarting monsters. Sometimes I returned to my home planet – once, even becoming president of my people to stop an invasion by two alien species. Then I took on a mission assigned to me by the White Guardian, a being even more powerful than my own people, to gather the six pieces of the Key to Time in order to restore balance to the cosmos.

> " If I kill, wipe out a whole intelligent lifeform, then I become like them. I'd be no better than the Daleks. "

Meanwhile, the Daleks were gathering strength. Recognising the Time Lords as their greatest enemy, the Daleks tried to use me and my friends in a plot to assassinate the Time Lords' High Council. I stopped that plot but was hardly taking sides – my relationship with my own people remained uneasy.

In fact, they deposed me as president and – despite all the missions I'd carried out on their instructions – put me on trial again for getting involved in the affairs of others! It turned out the charges were part of a conspiracy to hide the Time Lords' own murky dealings, and with the plot exposed, I was free to travel once more in space and time. Perhaps because the authority of my own people had been so undermined, I now stepped up my battle against evil. I took on various wicked gods and super-powerful beings, and set an elaborate trap for the Daleks.

They thought they were stealing a device that would make them as powerful as the Time Lords. But I had programmed it to destroy the Daleks' planet and star system. Some Daleks survived the loss of their home, and began to plot a terrible revenge …

THE TIME WAR RAGED between the Time Lords and the Daleks, at a terrible cost to the rest of the universe. Planets burned, or were wiped from existence. Whole civilisations were lost.

To begin with, I tried to stay out of the conflict. I flitted round helping people, as I always had. But when my help was scorned by **Cass** and then the Sisterhood of Karn petitioned me, I came to accept that I still had a vital role to play.

With the Sisterhood's help, I regenerated into a warrior, giving up the name "Doctor" and the promise it represented. I fought like a soldier – for many hard years – but could only see one way to stop the destruction and save the rest of the universe. I stole a Time Lord weapon known as the Moment. With it, I would destroy my home planet, all the Time Lords on it, and the Daleks too …

" Yes, I'm a Time Lord but I'm one of the nice ones. "

I didn't expect to survive, but I did. Utterly haunted by what I had done, I continued to travel, helping people in the shadow of the Time War.

After all I had lost, I was wary of making new friends, or of anything "domestic". But my friendship with **Rose Tyler** helped me to heal. When I lost Rose in another dimension, I made new friends – who, sadly, never stayed with me for long.

To my horror, I also learned that Daleks had survived the Time War, and were set on causing more havoc. I stood against them. When my own people threatened to return, I stood against them, too, and stopped the war beginning again, worse than ever before.

As the last of the Time Lords, I was sorely tempted to break all my people's old laws and interfere in history, saving lives where and when I chose – no matter the consequences to the universe as a whole. But in the end, I gave up my life to save an ordinary human being – an old man who was my friend.

I TRIED TO KEEP A LOW PROFILE in the universe. But the universe had other ideas.

There were the cracks in time and space that turned out to be the effect of my TARDIS exploding, sometime in the future. There was the kidnap of my companion, **Amy Pond**, and of *her* daughter (and my future wife), **River Song**. These things were the result of enemies in my future attacking my past.

I also had to deal with that momentous day in history when I'd ended the Time War. Teaming up with two previous incarnations, I finally learned that I *hadn't* reneged on my promise never to be cruel or cowardly, and had *not* destroyed my own people. Instead I – we – had saved them, but, because of the tangling of timelines with a swift regeneration thrown in, I'd buried the truth.

> ## " Never cruel or cowardly ...
> ## Never give up, never give in. "

Freed of that burden, I then spent a thousand years defending a small town of ordinary people on a planet where I knew I was destined to die. It proved to be this battle that prompted my enemies to attack my past. I stood my ground and defeated them, at the cost of yet another life.

I was haunted by past actions, and sometimes agonised over what to do when faced by evil. Rather than shoot Davros, creator of the Daleks, I taught him the importance of pity. I couldn't kill my wicked friend **Missy**, either, despite her many, heinous crimes. Instead, I became her guardian, and slowly changed her ways. And I didn't hesitate to give up my life to save people on a spaceship.

Now I'm more wide-eyed than ever at the universe around me. I've let go of the baggage that weighed down some of my earlier selves, travelling hopefully with my new gang around me. Well, you've got to be optimistic, haven't you? Every disaster's an opportunity to help, every danger brings new things to learn, so I just chuck myself in and hope for the best. Whatever comes, my story is only just beginning ... and it's going to be BRILLIANT!

HONOURABLE MENTIONS

ALICE AND MAY

PLAYED BY **Bridget Turner and Georgine Anderson**

OCCUPATION **Long-distance drivers**

FIRST APPEARANCE *Gridlock* (2007)

MARRIED COUPLE ALICE AND MAY were among the first drivers to get stuck in the gridlock of New Earth's motorway system, and continued to drive round it for the next 23 years. In all that time, they never saw a police car, ambulance or any kind of rescue vehicle but they held fast to their faith that they'd get out of the jam – and held on to their love for each other, too.

> **" You know full well we're not sisters, we're married. "**

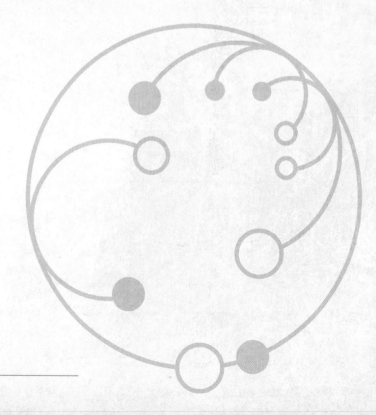

CARMEN

PLAYED BY **Ellen Thomas**

OCCUPATION **Low level psychic**

FIRST APPEARANCE *Planet of the Dead* (2009)

ONE EASTER EVENING, Carmen and her husband were on the
bus back home when the bus and everyone on it were swept through
a wormhole to the planet San Helios in the Scorpion Nebula.

" Death is coming. "

Ever since she was a girl, Carmen had had a psychic gift. She played the
National Lottery twice a week, each time correctly predicting three of the six
numbers and winning herself £10. Now the alien sun exacerbated her abilities.
She could vividly hear screaming – the voices of the dead of this world – and had
a premonition of the creatures that had killed them, and that were now racing
towards the bus. Her insights helped the Doctor work out what had happened,
and get the bus and its passengers back to Earth safely.

But Carmen had one last, ominous insight. She knew the Doctor was shortly
to die and shared with him a sinister foreshadowing of the event: *"He will knock
four times."*

CASS

PLAYED BY **Emma Campbell-Jones**

OCCUPATION **Gunship crewmember**

FIRST APPEARANCE *The Night of the Doctor* (2013)

CASS WANTED TO SEE THE UNIVERSE, so she joined the crew of a gunship. The ship was damaged in the Time War and sent crashing down towards the planet Karn. With the rest of the crew panicking and screaming, Cass calmly teleported them to safety and then sent a distress signal. When the Doctor arrived to rescue her in his TARDIS, Cass refused to go with him; in her eyes, Time Lords were no better than Daleks with the blood of billions on their hands. The Doctor tried to persuade her that he wasn't like other Time Lords, or even part of the Time War. But Cass preferred to crash and die than be saved by an "enemy" she so despised.

> " *I wanted to see the universe. Is it always like this?* "

THE GENERAL

PLAYED BY **T'Nia Miller**

OCCUPATION **Gallifreyan Military Commander**

FIRST APPEARANCE *Hell Bent* (2017)

THE GENERAL WAS THE MILITARY COMMANDER for the Gallifreyan Armed
Forces during and after the Last Great Time War. She was born female
and remained that way until she became a man in her eleventh incarnation.
She was happy to be a woman again when she regenerated into her twelfth
incarnation, wondering how men dealt with "all that ego".

> " *The only time I've been a man,
> that last body. Dear Lord, how
> do you cope with all that ego?* "

The newly regenerated General continued to chase the Doctor into the
Cloisters with **Ohila** to find out what he knew about the Hybrid. She was
compassionate and allowed his companion, **Clara**, to say some final words
to the Doctor before believing she would be returned to the point of her death.

GWEN COOPER

PLAYED BY **Eve Myles**

OCCUPATION **Police constable, Torchwood operative**

FIRST APPEARANCE *The Stolen Earth* (2008)

THERE WAS ONCE A WOMAN named Gwen who helped move an entire planet. Gwen worked for Torchwood, a crack team of investigators protecting the Earth from extra-terrestrial threats.

When the Earth was moved to the Medusa Cascade and invaded by Daleks, Gwen and her colleagues at the Torchwood Hub made contact with the Doctor. When a Dalek arrived at the Hub, Gwen knew that conventional weaponry would have no effect but picked up a gun anyway and said that she was going down fighting. She survived thanks to the Hub's time lock defence system which froze the Dalek in time. When the Daleks were eventually defeated, Gwen was able to help the Doctor return Earth to its original location by harnessing the power of the Rift, allowing him to tow it with his TARDIS.

HEATHER (THE PILOT)

PLAYED BY **Stephanie Hyam**

OCCUPATION **Student at St Luke's university**

FIRST APPEARANCE *The Pilot* (2017)

THERE WAS ONCE A YOUNG WOMAN who never felt happy in one place. Heather had a star in her eye, a defect in her left iris that meant she noticed something at once that regular people missed: an ordinary looking puddle did not reflect a mirror image. The puddle was in fact sentient oil left by a liquid spaceship. It was stranded on Earth with nowhere to go, until it found a new pilot in Heather. The Heather-Creature could now move anywhere in time and space but she was fixated on **Bill**, a canteen assistant she'd grown attracted to. She couldn't leave without her because Heather had made a promise to wait for her.

" Everywhere I go, I just want to leave ... "

Bill was able to free Heather by saying goodbye but this wouldn't be goodbye forever. Heather left some of her tears behind so that she could stay connected with Bill. Eventually, when Bill was converted into a Cyberman on a colony ship from Mondas, Heather tracked her down and turned her into an oil creature, like herself, so they could explore the universe together.

LORNA BUCKET

PLAYED BY **Christina Chong**

OCCUPATION **Soldier from the Gamma Forests**

FIRST APPEARANCE *A Good Man Goes to War* (2011)

ONCE, AN IMPRESSIONABLE YOUNG GIRL met the Doctor and was haunted by the encounter ever after. She and her people remembered him as a great warrior, so when Lorna set out to meet the Doctor again, it seemed logical to join an army – even one determined to kill him.

Once the army found him, Lorna switched sides, helping the Doctor and his friends, warning them of dangers and even embroidering a prayer leaf for his companion **Amy**'s new baby girl. Kind and brave, Lorna died fighting to protect that baby.

> " *I met you once, in the Gamma Forests. You don't remember me.* "

PRESIDENT OF EARTH

PLAYED BY **Vera Fusek**

OCCUPATION **President of Earth**

FIRST APPEARANCE *Frontier in Space* (1973)

ONCE UPON A TIME IN THE FUTURE, the President of Earth tried to prevent a war between her people and the Draconian Empire. She worked closely with the Draconian ambassador, and was even ready to listen to a strange man called the Doctor, who claimed that a wicked third party was engineering the conflict.

> " *If only we had proof. Then I could convince my people and you could convince yours.* "

For all she sought peaceful solutions, the President had a heart of steel. She was quick to order a complete security blackout in an attempt to keep bad news from her people, and kept thousands of critics of her government imprisoned on the Moon.

RODAN

PLAYED BY **Hilary Ryan**

OCCUPATION **Space Traffic Control technician**

FIRST APPEARANCE *The Invasion of Time* (1978)

THERE WAS ONCE A WOMAN who thought she had life easy. Rodan oversaw the transduction barriers that protected the planet Gallifrey from alien attack – which no alien would ever dare to do. Except then there *was* an invasion and, to her utter horror, Rodan found herself cast out of the calm and civilised Time Lord Citadel into the harsh outer world, without the most basic knowledge of how to survive. However, with the help of **Leela** she quickly rallied, not only joining the fight back against the aliens but helping to build the super-weapon that would ultimately defeat them.

> " *Do stop cavorting about like that. It's really so undignified.* "

URSULA BLAKE

PLAYED BY **Shirley Henderson**

OCCUPATION **Member of LInDA**

FIRST APPEARANCE *Love & Monsters* (2006)

THERE WAS ONCE A YOUNG WOMAN who took photographs during an alien invasion, and by chance got a picture of the mysterious Doctor. Ursula didn't understand the significance at first, but was soon invited to join the London Investigation 'n' Detective Agency. This group of friends didn't just investigate the Doctor; there was cooking, writing and music … and the stirrings of love.

> **"Use that cane on him and you'll get one hell of a smack off me! And then a good kick."**

Sadly, the group was taken over by a wicked alien who absorbed its members, including Ursula, into its body. Even so, she was clever enough to read the alien's thoughts and warn the man she loved – and fiercely protected – that it was after him next. Later, prompted by the Doctor, Ursula helped defeat the alien. She was left as just a face in a paving slab. But Ursula looked to the positive. She would never age, she felt quite peaceful, and the man she loved still loved her.

AND NOT FORGETTING ...

ABIGAIL – singer

ADRASTA – lady of Chloris

AIR DUCT – Red Kang gang member

ALICE O'DONNELL – systems technician

DR ALLISON WILLIAMS – physicist

ASTRID FERRIER – resistance leader

BELL – UNIT corporal

BIN LINER – Red Kang gang member

CAMECA – Aztec singleton

CAROL RICHMOND – astronaut

CONTROL – space traveller, cataloguer

COURTNEY WOODS – first woman on
the Moon and future US president

DELTA – Chimeron queen

ELIZABETH II – queen

ERICA – bacteriologist

EVELINA – psychic Roman

FARIAH – food taster, rebel

FIRE ESCAPE – Red Kang gang member

FLAVIA – Time Lord chancellor,
acting president

FLORENCE FINNEGAN – plasamvore

MS FOSTER – alien nanny

FRANCINE JONES – Martha's cross mum

DR GEMMA CORWYN – space station
second-in-command

GIA KELLY – manager, T-Mat Earth Control

GRACE O'BRIEN – brilliant nan

HAZRAN – colonist, mother

HILDA WINTERS – leader, Scientific
Reform Society

IRAXXA – Empress of Mars

ISOBEL WATKINS – photographer

JANE HAMPDEN – school teacher

JOURNEY BLUE – lieutenant, Combined
Galactic Resistance

KALA – conspirator, murderer

KARA – food manufacturer

MADAME KARABRAXOS – space bank
manager

KARRA – Cheetah person

KATH MCDONNELL – spaceship captain

KATRYCA – warrior queen

MADAME LAMIA – roboticist

LAVINIA SMITH – virologist

LEXA – religious leader

MA TYLER – psychic

MAAGA – Drahvin leader

MADELEINE ISSIGRI – mining
company chief

MAGAMBO – UNIT captain

MARILYN MONROE – movie star

MARY ASHE – space colonist

MINNIE HOOPER – minx

MIRANDA CLEAVES – acid miner

MORGAINE – warrior queen, witch

NANCY – Blitz survivor

NASREEN CHAUDHRY – mineralogist

NORNA – scientific assistant

PANNA – mystic

LADY PEINFORTE – sorceress

RACHEL "RAY" DEFWYDD – motor
mechanic

RACHEL JENSEN – scientific advisor

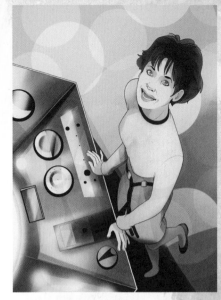

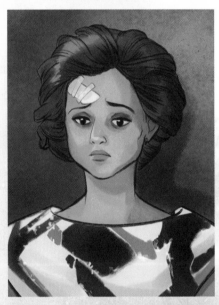

VERITY ANN LAMBERT

OCCUPATION **Producer**

An Unearthly Child (1963) – *Mission to the Unknown* (1965)

ONCE UPON A TIME, MANY YEARS AGO, there was a girl who insisted on doing her own thing.

Her name was aptly chosen – "Verity" means truth, and this only child was always honest and direct. Aged 10, she was sent to a smart new school, her parents hoping to turn her into lady. But the intelligent, well-read Verity later said she "couldn't knuckle under" to the strict regime. "My headmistress thought I was wilful."

Verity left school at 16 with fewer qualifications than her parents had hoped for. She took an arts diploma at the University of Paris, and returned to England to take a secretarial course.

This led to a job as a secretary at ABC Television, and she quickly fell in love with the busy, exciting medium. Soon she became a personal assistant, working with directors to ensure programmes ran smoothly – even when an actor suddenly died during a live production!

Yet Verity felt undervalued and considered quitting TV – until the head of drama at the BBC asked her to produce a new series he'd helped devise for children. At 28, Verity became the BBC's youngest ever and first female producer.

The programme was, of course, *Doctor Who*. Many at the BBC didn't want anything to do with a children's series, but Verity loved the idea and threw herself into the job, defying those who stood in her way. She cast William Hartnell as the Doctor, and battled her bosses when they objected to a story about machine creatures they dismissed as "bug-eyed monsters". The tenacious Verity got her way, and the Daleks made *Doctor Who* a huge ratings success.

The series made Verity a success too. She left after two years to produce other series, and was soon a head of drama herself, and then head of her own company, producing hit after hit – programmes that drew big audiences and won critical acclaim. She was truly remarkable. The Doctor, the Daleks and those first key years of *Doctor Who* were just some of her myriad, extraordinary achievements.

INDEX

WITH THANKS TO OUR WONDERFUL ILLUSTRATORS ...

ACKNOWLEDGEMENTS

Christel and Simon would like to thank the cast and crew of *Doctor Who*, past and present, for inspiration. Thanks also to Gabby and the team at Cardiff for their support and enthusiasm for this book.

We consulted former executive producer Russell T Davies on the name of **the Hostess** in *Midnight* and the identity of **the Woman** in *The End of Time*, and agreed with him that in both cases it was better to retain the mystery.

Former executive producer, Steven Moffat, told us that since writing *Hell Bent* he's come up with a name for **the General** – Kenossium – to be used in the *Doctor Who Magazine* comic strip (it's Latin for "Ken Bones", the actor who played the male incarnation of the character). We decided to stick with what's given on screen.

Lee Binding provided us with a close-up of **Yvonne Hartmann**'s ID badge, giving her official job title.

We drew from the archives of *Doctor Who Magazine*, as well as from *Doctor Who: The Shooting Scripts* (BBC Books, 2005) and Richard Marson's *Drama and Delight – The Life of Verity Lambert* (Miwk Publishing Ltd, 2015).

Thanks also to Heba Abd el Gawad, Samira Ahmed, Simon Belcher, Debbie Challis, James Cooray Smith, and to Paul Simpson for proofreading.

Thanks to Jim Smith for the wonderful design, and Lee Binding for the beautiful cover.

And to Beth, Tess, Sarah and Albert, and everyone at BBC Books, our editor Steve Cole for his brilliance, and to all the amazing illustrators.

1 3 5 7 9 10 8 6 4 2

BBC Books, an imprint of Ebury Publishing
20 Vauxhall Bridge Road,
London SW1V 2SA

BBC Books is part of the Penguin Random House group of companies
whose addresses can be found at global.penguinrandomhouse.com

Doctor Who is a BBC Wales production for BBC One.
Executive producer: Chris Chibnall

First published by BBC Books in 2018

www.penguin.co.uk

A CIP catalogue record for this book is available from the British Library

ISBN 9781785943591

Editorial Director: Albert DePetrillo
Project Editor: Steve Cole
Cover design: Lee Binding
Design: Jim Smith
Production: Phil Spencer

Printed and bound in Italy by L.E.G.O. S.p.A.

Penguin Random House is committed to a sustainable future for our business, our readers
and our planet. This book is made from Forest Stewardship Council® certified paper.